Against the Odds

The Jackie Joyner-Kersee Story
by Michele Spirn

AMSCO SCHOOL PUBLICATIONS, INC.
315 Hudson Street / New York, N.Y. 10013

Text Design by Merrill Haber

Cover Design by A Good Thing, Inc.

Compositor and Artwork: A Good Thing, Inc.

Please visit our Web site at:
   www.amscopub.com

When ordering this book, please specify:
   either **R 692 P** *or*
   AGAINST THE ODDS
   THE JACKIE JOYNER-KERSEE STORY

Amsco Originals

ISBN 1-56765-063-5
NYC Item 56765-063-4

Printed in the United States of America

1 2 3 4 5 6 7 8 9 10   04 03 02 01 00

Chapter 1

The First Lady of Something

When a little girl was born on March 3, 1962, the nation was filled with hope. John F. Kennedy was the youngest man ever to be elected president. He and his wife Jacqueline, or Jackie, as she was known, were adored for their youth, their good looks, and their fresh ideas about changing America.

At the time, many new babies were named after the president and his wife. Jackie Joyner was one. Her great-grandmother, Ollie Mae Johnson, named her, saying, "Someday, this little girl is going to be the first lady of something."

But while Jackie Kennedy had been born into wealth and privilege, Jackie Joyner was the child of poor parents. The Joyners were so poor that sometimes in the winter they had no heat; the whole family had to sleep near the stove to keep warm.

Often mayonnaise and bread was dinner; the children had to wear their shoes until the soles wore out.

Alfred and Mary Joyner, Jackie's parents, had married when they were very young. Mr. Joyner was 14 and Mrs. Joyner was 16 when Al, their first child, was born. Jackie came next. Then there were two sisters, Angela and Debra.

Mr. Joyner had to leave school to find work to support his family. He had been a good athlete, but he gave up sports to shine shoes, mow lawns, do odd jobs—anything to get money for his wife and children. Mary Joyner was a nurse's assistant at St. Mary's Hospital.

Later, Mr. Joyner got a job working as a railroad switch operator. But his job was two hours away, so he only came home on weekends.

Life was rough in East St. Louis. Factories closed and people lost their jobs. Some turned to crime, drugs, and violence. When Jackie was 11, she saw a man shot on the street. A year later, Jackie's grandmother called to say she would come to visit. The next morning, Jackie found out that her stepgrandfather had come home high on drugs and killed her grandmother.

There was one bright spot in the neighborhood: the Mary E. Brown Community Center. Children went there to dance, read, swim and play sports. When she was nine, Jackie signed up for track and field and dance lessons.

"At the time, dance was my first love. The instructor cared for me a lot and felt that one day I would be on Broadway."

She, her sisters and her friends formed a group, The Fabulous Dolls, to do dance routines. But her instructor died suddenly. Jackie was very upset and threw herself into sports instead.

She had a long way to go. The first time she ever ran a race she came in dead last. Although she won a ribbon for being in the race, Jackie was not pleased.

"I decided that this was a challenge and that I was going to do my best."

Soon Coach Nino Fennoy, who ran the Center's track program, began to notice this girl with the "skinny little legs . . . and the smile." He noticed her even more after a later track meet when she won five first-place awards.

"What stood out about her," he said, "was the happiness. She wanted to be doing what we were doing. . . . She came to practice. She had respect for adults and for discipline, and she had an air of enjoyment, like, 'My parents sent me here to have some fun and learn some things.' She wasn't in a hurry, she never complained."

At home, her brother Al, who was two years older, took notice of her, too. They were always very close, but they loved to tease each other.

Early on, Jackie began getting up at five A.M. to practice running. Al bragged that he could beat her in a race without practicing. Jackie took him up on it. She practiced every day.

The day of the big race came. Neighborhood kids lined up to watch the race. Many of them were Al's friends.

Jackie and Al raced from the mailbox at the corner of their street to the fence in front of the house. Jackie won.

"I felt kind of bad. I was a girl beating a boy, and Al's friends started calling him names. But by beating Al, I let him know that I wasn't a push-around. And he learned to respect me as an athlete."

For years, Jackie beat Al at everything they competed in. Even in basketball, Al had to be physically rough to win. Jackie became a role model for Al, even though he was older.

"I didn't have an older brother," he joked. "I had Jackie."

Jackie put all her energy into school and sports. Her mother, because of her own early marriage, said she would not allow her daughters to date until they were 18. All the children were expected to help with the housework and get good grades. For the girls, dates with boys were out of the question.

As her husband said, "If Mary said she wasn't going to move on something, she wasn't going to move."

"My mother was the foundation," Jackie said. "She didn't want us to be like her—not getting what she wanted because she couldn't go to college. She wanted us to find a way out."

So Jackie spent a lot of time with Coach Fennoy, improving her skills and her mind. He made her keep journals on the track team's road trips. He corrected them for grammar and spelling.

"Where you're going, you'll need to express yourself with more than arms and legs," he said.

He began training Jackie for the 400-meter run. Jackie really wanted to try the long jump.

"He had other girls jumping, and I just had to sit around and wait. One day, a young lady was late to practice, so I just ran down the runway and jumped."

The coach was amazed. Jackie had jumped almost 17 feet—as far as a high school athlete.

"Can you do that again?" he asked. She did.

The coach looked at her. "You've been this good all this time."

Later, Jackie said, "It was something I had always wanted to do, and it was taken away from me, and I got a chance by accident. The following year, I set a record of 17 feet for 12- and 13-year-olds."

As always, Jackie practiced her new skill. Al and her sisters brought home sand in potato chip bags. They used the sand to make a landing pit at the end of their porch.

But Coach Fennoy had bigger plans for Jackie. He saw that Jackie was good at running and jumping. He saw that she also loved to play basketball and volleyball. He decided that she was a good natural all-around athlete. She was perfect for the pentathlon.

The pentathlon was an Olympic event for women. There were five parts to it: an 800-meter race, hurdles, the shot put, the long jump, and the high jump. Coach Fennoy thought that Jackie would have a big head start at winning the pentathlon because she was such a good runner and jumper.

He was right. In 1976, Jackie tried out and qualified for the pentathlon at the National Junior Olympics. There was only one problem: money. Jackie and her teammates didn't have the money to pay for the long car trip. Their parents couldn't afford it. So the girls decided to raise money. They sold candy. They held bake sales. They saved what they could. Finally, they had enough money to go.

Jackie won the pentathlon with the highest score in her age group. She began to dream about a future in sports. She started reading about women athletes and found one who inspired her: Wilma Rudolph.

It would be a struggle to have a career like Wilma's. But Jackie was on her way.

SIDEBAR #1: OLYMPIC WOMEN

Wilma Rudolph: The Chattanooga Choo Choo

They called her "The Tennessee Tornado" or the "Chattanooga Choo Choo" after the high-speed train from her home state, Tennessee.

Yet, before track star and Olympic gold medalist Wilma Rudolph was eight, most people thought she'd never walk again.

Wilma was born on June 23, 1940, in Clarksville, Tennessee. She was the 20th of 22 children fathered by Ed Rudolph, a railway porter, in two marriages. She was so tiny—four pounds—that they weren't sure whether she would live. She did but later caught double pneumonia and scarlet fever. Her left leg became paralyzed, and doctors thought she might never be able to use it.

But Wilma and her mother were determined that she would walk. Each week, her mother would wrap Wilma in a blanket and travel 90 miles to a free hospital clinic so doctors could take care of Wilma. There, Wilma's mother learned how to rub and massage her leg four times a day. She taught Wilma's brothers and sisters to do it too.

Wilma had to sit all day in a special chair. Yet, her mother said, "It didn't make her cross. She tried to play. The other children came and played with her while she sat in the chair."

Others might not have believed it, but Wilma never lost hope that one day she would be able to walk. When she was eight, with the help of a special shoe, she took her first steps.

At 13, she was able to run, and in high school she started to show her athletic talent. For five years in a row, Wilma won every dash race she entered in Tennessee. She became an All-State basketball player, scoring 803 points in 25 games for her school in 1956.

Wilma Rudolf at the 1960 Olympics in Rome, Italy

At Tennessee State University, she began to work hard on outdoor track with Coach Clinton Gray. Wilma told her friends that she hoped to become America's most famous woman runner. Many wondered whether a girl who had been disabled could do it.

She showed them. At the Olympic Games in Rome in 1960, Wilma won the 100-meter race, breaking a record, the 200-meter race, and the 400-meter women's relay race. She became the first American woman to win three gold medals in a single Olympics.

In 1961, she was the first African-American woman to win the James E. Sullivan Memorial Trophy, given to the athlete who best advanced the cause of sportsmanship. In the same year, she was asked to be the first woman in 30 years to run in the most famous of all indoor track meets, the Millrose Games. Cheered on by a mostly male audience, Wilma won the 60-yard dash in 6.9 seconds, tying her own world record.

"When I was running, I had the sense of freedom, of running in the wind," she said. "I never forgot all the years when I was a little girl and not able to be involved in sports. When I ran, I felt like a butterfly. That feeling was always there."

SIDEBAR #2: NEEDING TO WIN

Sprinting

Among the different skills Jackie Joyner-Kersee needed to work on to win the Olympics was sprinting. Sprinting is running, but it's more than just being fast. Sprinters have to be strong. They also have to be able to relax when they run.

Jackie had to learn how to sprint for two kinds of races—the 200-meter dash and the 400-meter race. In the 200, the runners start just before a curve.

They have to run around another curve to finish the race. In the 400, they have to go around the track completely.

Although she was born a fast runner, Jackie had to learn a few things to be able to sprint to win. At some point in the race, she had to run a little slower, then speed up. Most sprinters speed up at the end of the race.

She had to learn to lean her body forward at the end of the race. The sprinter who breaks the tape first at the end of the race wins. The tape has to be broken by your upper body. Jackie learned to lean forward at the end of the race to give her an advantage.

Building up her body was another thing Jackie learned. Being strong can give you a powerful start at the beginning of the race. That's why Jackie does 500 sit-ups, lifts 220 pounds and works out for eight hours a day.

Chapter 2

High School Lessons

In the 1977 Junior Olympics, Jackie won the pentathlon again. People started talking about her. She won the pentathlon so far ahead of any other competitor that her photo and name appeared in *Sports Illustrated*'s "Faces in the Crowd" section.

By 1979, Jackie had won four Junior Olympics pentathlons in a row. No one else could match her.

At Lincoln High School, she trained with Coach Fennoy, who was in charge of track and field, and joined the basketball and volleyball teams. Jackie gave up her part-time job at a movie theater and left the cheerleading team. She decided to focus on two things: her studies and sports.

It was a smart decision. Coach Fennoy had helped many other young athletes win college scholarships. He helped Jackie work toward her goals of college and a career as an athlete.

Not that everything always went so smoothly for Jackie.

In the 1977–78 season, the Lincoln basketball team was so good, it was expected to win the Illinois state finals. But first came the semi-finals. Lincoln was playing Centralia High. Everyone thought Lincoln was sure to win.

In fact, Lincoln had a strong lead over Centralia. Then, in the middle of the game, the lights went out in the gym.

Because the Lincoln team thought they would win, they passed the time until the lights were fixed by fooling around and talking. Meanwhile, the Centralia team exercised and talked about how they would play the game after the lights came back on.

When the gym was lit again, the Centralia team came roaring back, scoring quickly. Jackie and her teammates were so surprised they started playing badly. They stopped playing as a team. They took bad shots and didn't pay attention to each other.

Centralia won. Lincoln lost not only the game, but their heart for playing. They had trouble for the rest of the year.

That game taught Jackie the importance of teamwork and what it meant to be a leader.

"I learned to ask myself whether I was doing the things that were in my best interest and in the best interest of the team. And I learned that as a leader I had to be willing to make the same demands on my teammates."

Jackie's demands as a leader didn't always make her popular.

"Sometimes my teammates would get mad at me or tease me because I confronted them or told the coach if I thought someone was doing something that could stop the team from winning, like hanging out with a boyfriend instead of going to practice. That didn't make me too popular at first, but after a while my teammates respected me for doing it. They knew that it would help us become champions."

In her senior year, Jackie was captain of the basketball team. That year Lincoln won the state finals.

People paid attention to Jackie when she played basketball. In one game, in the last second of play, she made a shot from 25 feet away to win the game.

"Jackie Joyner is the finest athlete in the state of Illinois," one sportswriter wrote after seeing her play basketball.

Yet, she was also human. Once her friend Carmen Cannon-Taylor asked Jackie to cut a training run short. Coach Fennoy had asked them to take a practice run around town because Lincoln High School had no track. The route they were to run passed right in front of Carmen's house.

As they passed Carmen's house, she told Jackie that they could stop and have one of Jackie's favorite sandwiches: ham with lettuce, pickles and mayonnaise. Jackie couldn't help herself. The girls stopped and had sandwiches. Then they took a shortcut back to the school.

No one would have ever known. But that

night Jackie felt bothered. She called Carmen up. They went out in the dark to run the part of the course they had missed. But Jackie did better than that. She insisted they run the whole course all over again.

"She was the captain of the team," Carmen said. " . . . if you do 100 percent, she'll do 120 percent. We were all disciplined, but she was more disciplined."

"I kept saying to myself, 'I've got to work hard, I've got to be successful,'" Jackie said.

When she was 16, she got carried away playing basketball one night. It was after 11 P.M. Her mother had told her she had to be home once the streetlights came on. Mary Joyner went down to the community center.

"She ran over with a switch in her hand," Jackie said. "She beat me all the way home with that switch."

Jackie's hard work made Al sit up and take notice. He was a senior in high school and a good triple jumper, not a great one. But the triple jump was his chance for an athletic scholarship to college. Jackie kept telling him he needed to practice more. She woke him up early in the morning. She told him to go out and train. She told him that if he would practice more and train hard enough, he would get that scholarship.

In the last three weeks of his senior year, Al had improved his personal best to over 50 feet in the triple jump. The coach at Tennessee State

University took a look at Al and offered him a scholarship.

Jackie, too, was improving. She was named All-State and All-America in track and basketball. In the spring of her junior year, she long jumped a state high school record: 20' 7½".

By this time, Jackie was too advanced for the Junior Olympics. In 1980, she was asked to try out for the Olympics in the long jump. Rarely was a high school student invited to try out. Jackie was thrilled.

She jumped a personal best of 20' 9¾", but it wasn't good enough to make the team. Only the top three contestants make the team, and Jackie finished eighth.

But in 1980, no American athletes went to the Summer Olympic Games. The games were held in Moscow, Russia. The Soviet Union, of which Russia was part of in 1980, had invaded the country of Afghanistan. War was going on between the Soviets and the people of Afghanistan. Many countries, including the U.S., thought this invasion of Afghanistan was wrong and an act against international law. They thought that by invading Afghanistan, the Soviets were not living up to the ideals of the Olympics. How could countries participate in the Olympics when the host had gone into another country and started a war? Wasn't the Olympics supposed to be about peace and countries learning how to get along?

After much discussion, U.S. President Jimmy Carter decided that it would be wrong to send American athletes to the Summer Olympics. He announced that the United States would withdraw from the competition.

Jackie had other things to think about. She had graduated from her class in the top ten percent. Because she had such good grades and a great athletic record, she was offered many college scholarships. Most of them were for basketball.

She really wanted a track-and-field scholarship, but those were much harder to get. At that time, she was also more of a star in basketball than she was in track and field.

Jackie decided that the first step would be to get to college on a scholarship. Once she was there, she would see what she could do to get what she really wanted.

Her biggest problem was deciding where to go. No one else in her family, except for Al, had gone to college. Jackie had to make the choice herself. Three things helped her decide.

Basketball coach Billie Moore of the University of California in Los Angeles (UCLA) came to visit Jackie four times to try and get her to choose UCLA. UCLA's basketball team was one of the best in the country. And, finally, UCLA was known for its fine coaches. Jackie knew that only the best could help her get where she wanted to go—to the Olympics.

Before she said "yes" to Coach Moore, Jackie asked her if she could go out for the women's track and field team. Coach Moore agreed as long as track meets and practices didn't get in the way of basketball games and drills.

Track was still Jackie's first love. So in the fall of 1980, Jackie left the little house on Piggott Street next to the pool hall and the liquor store in East St. Louis and traveled to a city filled with smog, palm trees, movie stars—and most important—plenty of chances for a young, promising athlete.

Jackie and her brother Al and the house they lived in as children

17

"I remember Jackie and me crying together in a back room of the house, swearing that someday we were going to make it," Al said. "Make it out. Make things different."

Now both Al and Jackie were on their way.

SIDEBAR #3: TALKING TRACK

Decathlon – An Olympic event with ten parts: 100-meter, 400-meter, and 1,500-meter runs; the 110-meter high hurdles; the javelin and discus throws; the shot put, pole vault, high jump, and long jump.

Foul – Stepping on or beyond the line allowed during the run-up or approach before running, jumping, or throwing. When an athlete fouls, the jump, run, or throw is not counted.

Hamstring – Any of three muscles at the back of the thigh.

High jump – The jumper has to clear a bar set across poles. After 1968, high-jumpers jumped head first over the bar like American Dick Fosbury, who won the Olympic gold medal that year. He made the "Fosbury flop" famous.

Hurdles – Obstacles a runner has to jump or step over. In the outdoor Olympic races, hurdlers have to clear 10 hurdles.

Long-distance races – Races of more than 2,000 meters.

Marathon – The longest race in the Olympics—26 miles, 385 yards.

Middle-distance races – Races from 800 meters to 2,000 meters.

Pentathlon – An Olympic event with five parts, designed for women. In 1984, it was replaced by the heptathlon.

Personal best – The best an athlete can do in his sport, such as his shortest race time, longest throw, or highest point total.

Sprints – Short races up to 400 meters.

Triple jump – A field event. The athlete finishes three jumps in one try, first landing on the take-off foot, then on the other foot, and then with both feet in the sand pit.

SIDEBAR #4: WHAT IS THE HEPTATHLON?

When Jackie Joyner competed in the heptathlon in 1984, it was the first Olympics for the new event. Two new events—the javelin and the 200-meter race—had been added to the pentathlon, or five-event competition, to make seven events. "Hept" means "seven" in Greek. The heptathlon lasts for two days.

First Day

1. *100-meter hurdles* – The athletes race 100 meters while stepping over ten hurdles, which

are three feet high. If an athlete knocks over a hurdle, she loses no points.

2. *High jump* – Athletes try to jump over a crossbar balanced on two poles. Each time an athlete clears the crossbar, it is raised. Each jumper gets three tries at each height.

Jackie showing great running form

3. *Shot put* – Each athlete lifts an 8-pound 13-ounce metal ball. The ball is the "shot." The athlete holds the shot at her shoulder, pushes it away from her body, and throws it. All the while, the athlete has to stay in a circle, which is seven feet in diameter.

4. *200-meter dash* – Athletes sprint one-half of a 400-meter track.

Second Day

5. *Long jump* – Athletes take a running start and jump for distance. Jumpers have to stay behind a take-off board before jumping. The distance is measured from the board to the first mark the jumper makes in the sand when she lands.

6. *Javelin throw* – Holding a pointed spear called a javelin, the athlete runs and throws it for distance.

7. *800-meter race* – The final event has the athletes run two laps or twice around a 400-meter track.

Chapter 3

Troubles at School,
Troubles at Home

In her first year at UCLA, the star from East St. Louis became just one of many talented athletes. UCLA was full of them.

Jackie had her hands full. First, she decided to study history. UCLA was not the kind of school that lets athletes skip their academic work for sports. Jackie had plenty of reading and writing to do.

Next, she got off to a slow start in basketball, her scholarship sport.

"She's fast and she's wild," said one fan.

Soon, however, Jackie started doing better. She was a four-year starter for her team, the Bruins, and a player in every game. Playing center forward, her favorite position, Jackie was great at making points, rebounding, or catching the ball after it bounced off the backboard or basketball hoop, and good at assists—helping other players score.

Coach Moore was pleased with Jackie.

"All the old-fashioned words apply to Jackie," she said. "Dedication, discipline, hard work."

Jackie was happy, but she still longed for the track and the long jump.

Her third problem was her basketball scholarship. Because of it, the track and field coaches thought of her as a basketball player. In their words, she was a "walk-on"—someone who had some talent in track and field but who was more serious about another sport. They thought that a walk-on wouldn't spend the necessary time to improve her skills in another sport. They thought she didn't care enough to work hard or practice.

Jackie wasn't even sure of where to start. All her life, she had worked with one coach—Nino Fennoy. He was the only one she had to impress. Now she looked around and saw that UCLA had many coaches. Some of them tried to help her, but they were too busy to spend much time with her. They had no idea of what she could do.

Often, she would get advice from one coach one day. The next day, she would get completely different advice from another coach. Jackie didn't know what to do. She was too shy and polite to say anything. So she started doing what she had always done, practicing by herself. She jumped over and over again, trying to get better. She only got worse.

But one coach started to notice her. That was Bob Kersee.

Bob Kersee

"I saw this talent walking around the campus that everyone was blind to. No one was listening to her mild requests to do more," he said.

Bob was new to UCLA too. He had come there in 1980 to be the new assistant coach for women sprinters and hurdlers. He was not a long-jump coach, but he saw something in Jackie. Bob knew she could be a great long jumper. He knew her problem was not lack of talent, but lack of technique.

Jackie had noticed Bob also. At first, "I only knew him as this coach who was always screaming like a madman at his athletes." But she also wished that she had a coach who cared enough about her to yell at her.

Bob began working with Jackie and realized that she was more talented than he had thought. He decided that instead of just concentrating on the long jump, she should train for a multievent, or a sport that had more than one part to it—the heptathlon.

There was no special coach at UCLA then for multievents, so Bob had to ask the women's athletic director, Dr. Judith Holland, if it was all right for him to take this on along with all the other coaching he was doing.

He later said he told Dr. Holland about Jackie, "Either I coached her in the hurdles, long jump and multievents, or I'd quit because to go on as she had would be an abuse of her talent."

Jackie was more than interested in this new

Olympic event. She liked the idea of a challenge. The long jump meant a lot of waiting in between jumps. There would be a lot more action with the heptathlon. There was no Olympic basket-ball event for women. So the heptathlon might be the event that would get her to the Olympics.

By the time Christmas came around, Jackie had settled in at UCLA and was looking forward to the new year. Her mother asked her to come home for the holidays, but Jackie had made a lot of new friends and wanted to stay in California. It was her first time living away from home, and she thought she was "too independent now." She promised her mother she would come home for spring break, just a few months away.

But in January, 1981, Jackie got a call from home. Her mother had come down with a rare disease. Both Jackie and Al, who had changed colleges and was now at Arkansas State, rushed home.

Mary Joyner was in a coma. She was not awake, and could not speak to any of her family. Doctors told Jackie, Al, their two sisters, their father, and their aunt, Della Gaines, that Mary Joyner would never wake up. The disease had destroyed her brain. They would be able to keep her alive with machines, but she would never be herself again.

Mrs. Joyner's doctors left it up to the family as to what they wanted to do. Mary Joyner had said that she never wanted to be kept alive by machines. But Mr. Joyner said he could not face giving the order to turn them off. He left the decision up to Al and Jackie.

The family prayed together. Then Jackie decided.

"If we'd left her on the machines, she'd never have known us, and she would have continued suffering indefinitely."

Jackie told the doctors to end her mother's pain and turn off the machines.

At the funeral, one of Jackie's sisters fainted. Jackie felt that she could not show her sadness. She had to be the strong one for the family.

"With her gone, some of her determination passed on to me," Jackie said.

Her Aunt Della took charge of Jackie's two sisters so Jackie and Al could go back to school.

At first, back at school, Jackie felt there was no one she could share her feelings with. She kept her sadness inside and tried not to show it.

But help came from Bob Kersee, who had heard about her mother's death. He was able to understand how she was feeling. He, too, had lost his mother when he was only 18 years old. He also worried that Jackie might feel she had to drop out of school and take care of her sisters now that she was the oldest woman in the family.

"I tried to protect her from the 'Now I'm the mom' syndrome,' " he said.

Jackie, who had only known him as a tough coach who yelled at his athletes, was surprised.

"I found it amazing because I didn't know him beyond his being a coach. But he said if I had doubts and need to talk them out, I could come to him."

He told Jackie that her mother would have wanted her to stay in school, and soon Jackie came to believe him.

"I found that I could talk to him about anything and everything," she said.

New training took her mind off her sadness and her worries about her family. With seven different events to practice, Jackie was busy. She was good at jumping, sprinting, and hurdling, but she needed a lot of practice in the 800-meter and the shot put. And the first time she tried to throw the javelin, she hit herself in the head.

Even though she was not good in all seven events, the heptathlon was made for Jackie. Because each of the events was scored for the total, Jackie didn't have to win each one. She might do just all right in the javelin, for instance, but very well in the long jump. Her score for the long jump would make up the difference.

Before Bob started coaching her, Jackie depended on her natural ability and her feelings to win. He showed her how to think about winning. Bob taught her how to decide where she might get the most points, how to make the most of her strengths, and how to improve her weaknesses. He told her where she had to work extra hard, and he made sure she did it.

"He was always yelling, telling me I was lazy and that I had a lot of talent, but I had to give it time to develop," she said. "I saw that he was bringing out the best in me."

With her determination, talent, and Bob Kersee's coaching, Jackie was about to take the first test of her new life as a heptathlete.

SIDEBAR #5: OLYMPIC MEN

Coach: The Bob Kersee Story

In October, 1988, Pat Jordan wrote about Bob Kersee in Life magazine: "His genius is in recognizing raw talent and channeling it in its natural direction."

Bob was born in Panama. His mother was from Panama, his father an American navy officer. In the U.S., the family moved from state to state because of his father's career.

When he was growing up, Bob's hero was Vince Lombardi, a famous football coach.

"Even as a kid, I studied track from a coach's point of view," he said. "I dreamed of being the first black coach in the National Football League, then the Olympic coach, and finally, I cut that down and started coaching Olympic athletes."

He graduated from Long Beach State in 1976 and was studying for his master's degree at Cal State-Northridge when he left to take the job of his childhood dreams—assistant track coach at UCLA. Not only did Bob know how to train athletes, he also knew how to get them to think about competing. He helped them improve by telling them how good they could be.

As Jackie's coach, he helped her set her goals. "It takes a lot of time, a lot of juggling, a lot of organization, and a lot of detail work trying to figure out which event to work on first, what each event should be focused on. And we just work day by day, week by week, trying to get all these little things down."

Bob Kersee should know. By 1984, he had helped seven athletes win 10 Olympic medals.

SIDEBAR #6: NEEDING TO WIN

High Jumping

In 1932, famed woman athlete Babe Didrikson Zaharias had the gold medal in the high jump taken away from her for jumping head first over the crossbars. But since 1968, that has been the way most high-jumpers go over the bar.

That style became famous when Dick Fosbury of the United States used it at the Olympic Games in Mexico City. Dick jumped 7' 4¼", and soon most jumpers began using the "Fosbury flop," as it became known.

The way Jackie and most other high-jumpers do it, is to get up speed by running. Then they jump head first over the bar and land on their shoulders.

A few jumpers still use the "straddle" jump— popular before the Fosbury flop. An athlete will bring her leg up toward the crossbar, then go over the bar face forward. Then she will land on her side or her back.

If Jackie or her competitors knock the bar off when jumping, that is a miss. Anyone who misses three times in a row is out of the competition. If there is a tie, the person with the least amount of misses wins.

The Fosbury Flop

Chapter 4

Not Their Time

Bob showed Jackie what good coaching could do when she competed in her first heptathlon at the Association of Intercollegiate Athletics for Women national championships in 1981.

The championships were held in Tacoma, Washington. At first, Jackie was going alone. When Bob found out that no coach had been assigned to go with her, he was angry. He said he would go even if he had to pay his own way. Finally, UCLA agreed to pay for Bob to go. It was a good thing they did.

Jackie didn't expect to do well. She was in her first year of college, competing for the first time in an event that was new to her.

After the first day of competition, Jackie knew she wasn't doing well. She was way behind in her point total. But Bob had an idea.

He decided that she could improve her long jump—already one of her best events. Instead of letting Jackie go to bed and rest, he turned the hallway of the motel where they were staying into a runway for the long jump. Using masking tape, he marked where Jackie would approach the jump and where she would take off. He made Jackie practice again and again.

The next day, Jackie jumped 21 feet. It was her best jump since high school. It helped Jackie get enough points to finish third in the competition.

Jackie felt better about herself and the heptathlon. She knew she was doing well in basketball, but she still wanted to do better in track. Bob wanted to help her because he believed in her. Even when she was behind after the first day of the heptathlon competition, he said, "Girl, you have a lot of talent. You're going to be one of the best heptathletes."

One day he showed her on paper how she had to improve. He wrote down her scores in each of the events. Then he showed her the winning scores. Suddenly, Jackie understood what she needed to do and where she needed to work on her weaknesses.

"Jane Frederick [then the best American heptathlete] was beating me by 400 points in just two events, the shot put and the javelin," she said.

Bob also showed her that she needed to work on the hurdles. She still didn't know how best to use her speed and her legs.

In the middle of her second year at UCLA, Jackie started improving. To help with her training program, Bob took Jackie to see Bob

Forster, a Los Angeles physical therapist with a fine reputation who said:

"She was like a gem in the raw. After examining her, though, I told him [Bob Kersee]: 'This girl's the real thing.'"

Suddenly, Jackie started to have breathing problems. During her workouts, she would have to stop, bend over and gasp for air. She was worried.

"I was in the emergency room every week," she said. "But I lived in denial. I wouldn't admit to myself: 'There's something wrong with you, girl.'"

Finally, the doctors told Jackie she had asthma. Although asthma can be caused by many things, in Jackie's case they thought it was brought on by so much exercise. They told her that medicine would help her asthma, but it would never go away completely. Jackie listened and learned how to take her medicine and rest when an attack came on. She would learn to manage her asthma, not let it manage her.

In fact, the asthma did not slow her down. In her second year at UCLA, when the track team won the National Collegiate Athletic Association (NCAA) championship, Jackie had scored 32 of the team's 153 winning points.

She had started training as a heptathlete in 1981. Less than a year later, she won the NCAA heptathlon championship and set a record of 6,099 points to become the top collegiate heptathlete. As if that record wasn't enough, Jackie went on to win the Athletics Congress national championship in the heptathlon. The Athletics Congress makes the rules and has control over all the track and field events in the U.S. Jackie was now ranked as the best heptathlete in the country.

Other sports were still important to Jackie. She also competed in the Athletic Congress national championship long jump. Just missing winning, she came in second. UCLA recognized her unusual abilities in basketball and track and field and named her All-University Athlete.

But despite her busy schedule on the track, in the classroom, and on the basketball court, she stayed in touch with her family. She was still very close to Al. Because they were both track and field athletes, they sometimes found themselves at the same event. Often, each one knew what the other was thinking without saying a word.

"We've got a special kind of ESP," Al said.

Al and Jackie were very happy when they both made the U.S. team for the World Championships in Helsinki, Finland, in the summer of 1983. Although winners do not get medals at the World Championships, the event plays an important part in sports competition. Winners are called world champions. And the competition itself, held every four years, is an important step in getting ready for the Olympics.

Both Al and Jackie were ready. But although athletes can train and practice for a long time before a competition and think they are ready for anything, surprises can happen.

Al thought he would do well. But he pulled a hamstring muscle. He could not jump his best. He tried, but he came in eighth.

Strangely enough, Jackie had the same thing happen. Usually, she kept ice on her hamstring muscles between events. She always did it at night after the first day's events. This time she forgot.

When she woke up in the morning, her legs were sore, and they hurt. Jackie tried to warm up. She did her exercises the way she always did. This time, her sore muscles did not loosen up. She pulled a hamstring too. She could not compete in the second day's events, and she had to withdraw.

Disappointed, brother and sister went home. But Al said something that made them both feel a little better.

"Jackie, it's just not our time yet," he said.

Jackie knew he was right. There was always another competition ahead. Most exciting of all, the 1984 Olympics was coming up.

SIDEBAR #7: THE OLYMPICS

The first Olympics, in Greece in 776 B.C., had only one event—a race. It was won by Coroebus of Elis, a cook. He received an olive wreath. His name, his father's name and his country's name were shouted out.

Rafer Johnson lights the Olympic rings at the 1984 Olympics.

Early Olympics were more religious festivals for Greeks than games or contests. Later Olympics became tests of strength and skill.

As events such as boxing, pentathlon, wrestling, and chariot racing were added, poems were written about the winner. Sculptors made life-size statues of them. They were given money and presents.

Athletes like Milo of Croton, who won the wrestling crown six times, became heroes. It was said that Milo became strong by carrying a calf on his shoulders daily until it grew to be a bull.

In A.D. 394, the Emperor Theodosius stopped the Olympics. He thought the games were too tied up with worshipping pagan gods. In 1892, Baron Pierre de Coubertin, a Frenchman, suggested the Olympics be started again. He thought athletics were important and that the Olympics would help nations cooperate and learn to live peacefully with each other.

"The important thing in the Olympic Games is not to win but to take part, just as the most important thing in life is not the triumph but the struggle. The essential thing is not to have conquered but to have fought well . . . ," he said.

Today's Olympics are held once every two years. At every opening ceremony, the Olympic flag is raised, and the flame, carried from Olympia, Greece, is used to light the torch. The torch burns until the last event is over.

SIDEBAR #8: ATHLETES AND ASTHMA

Asthma is a disease that causes problems with breathing. When a person has an asthma attack, he often feels as if he can't get enough air into his lungs. When he does breathe, he sometimes hears whistling sounds or wheezing coming from his chest. Sometimes, asthmatics cough a lot during attacks.

Some doctors think asthma is caused by dust or pollution in the air. Some believe that people who are allergic may be more likely to get asthma. In some cases, like Jackie's, asthma is brought on by a lot of exercise. Colds, infections, or certain foods can bring it on, too.

Jackie is not the only world-class athlete with asthma. Others who have it include the champion diver Greg Louganis and swimmer Nancy Hogshead.

Many years ago, people thought that children with asthma needed clean air to breathe. Many were sent away to the mountains to recover. Others thought that children with asthma shouldn't exercise or play sports. They should sit and watch.

Today, people who have asthma can and do exercise. There are many medications to help them. One of the problems with athletes taking medicine for asthma is that the Olympics have strict rules about taking certain drugs. Some asthma medicines contain these drugs. Jackie needs these drugs to breathe, but she does not take them for weeks before the Olympics because it can take weeks for her body to get rid of the drugs.

In 1972, Rick DeMont, a sixteen-year-old high school senior from California, won the 400-meter freestyle swimming race at the Munich Olympics. But he was disqualified when a banned drug, ephedrine, was found when he was tested. The drug was from his asthma medicine.

Rick tried to explain, but he had to give back his gold medal, and was not allowed to swim in the 1,500-freestyle.

That's one reason why Jackie won't take her asthma medicine before she competes and why she sometimes finishes races on her hands and knees, trying to get air into her lungs.

Chapter 5

1984

In 1983, Bob had a plan. He told Jackie she should sit out the year in college basketball and track. He thought she should do two things instead: go to class and train for the long jump and the heptathlon.

Although Jackie had a basketball scholarship, it allowed her to complete college in five years rather than four. She could take one year off from basketball under NCAA rules. She decided to do it.

Coach Billie Moore agreed. "If I coached another 40 years, I don't think I could find someone else like Jackie. She's a winner and a competitor. She knows how to prepare and what it takes to win . . . . But as great an athlete as she is, she's an even greater human being."

To make things even easier for Jackie, the Olympics was going to be held in Los Angeles, a city in which she was at home. Jackie wouldn't have to train for an unfamiliar place. The competition was supposed to be easier as well. To get back at the U.S. for not coming to the Summer 1980 Games in Moscow, the Soviet Union and its allies, including East Germany and Cuba, chose not to come to Los Angeles. The East German athletes were then thought to be the best heptathletes in the world. Everyone was betting on Jackie.

Los Angeles, 1984: The 8,000 athletes from 140 countries watched eagerly as Rafer Johnson lifted the Olympic torch. He had won the 1960 decathlon Olympic gold medal. Now Rafer had been given the honor of lighting the Olympic rings, opening the 23rd Olympic Games. As the rings burst into flame, the athletes cheered.

No one was more excited than Jackie. She had dreamed of going to the Olympics ever since she was 14 and had watched TV when Bruce Jenner won the gold in the decathlon in Montreal, Canada, in 1976.

"One day I'm going to go to the Olympics," she had said then to Al. Now she was here. Best of all, Al was in the Olympics too. Both Jackie and Al would be competing on the same day, at the same time—Jackie in the heptathlon, Al in the triple jump.

Both had made it against incredible odds. But in spite of everything, Jackie had a plan. She called it her "three D's"—determination, dedication and desire.

Determination: Jackie trained eight hours a day. Her coach, Bob Kersee, demanded hard work. He

Bruce Jenner at the 1976 Olympics shot put event

told Jackie to run up and down hundreds of steps. She lifted weights to build up her strength for the javelin throw and the shot put.

Dedication: Late in 1983, when Jackie found out she had asthma, her doctors told her if she cut down on her practice, it would help cut down on her asthma attacks. But Jackie was dedicated to the heptathlon and the long jump. Instead, she took medicine and rested when she felt an attack coming on. But at each competition, each race, each long jump, she lived with the fear that asthma might overcome her.

Desire: Jackie wanted nothing more than to be an Olympic champion. When she complained to Bob Kersee that he was working her too hard, he said, "Do you want to win the gold or the silver medal?" Jackie went back to practice.

The plan had taken her to the Olympics. Now, on August 4, Jackie walked onto the field in her red, white, and blue uniform. Although she had hurt the hamstring muscle at the back of her left leg, she was smiling. She was the favorite to win. Her fans called, "Jackie! Jackie!" and stamped their feet.

She had gone through two difficult days of Olympic trials to get there. All American competitors in every event have to go through the trials. The top three in each event compete for the U.S. at the Olympics.

Jackie competed against some great women in the trials. There was Jane Frederick, the record holder. At age 32, it was probably Jane's last time to make the team and compete in the heptathlon. Jodi Anderson, Cindy Greiner, and Patsy Walker were all experienced in the heptathlon.

In the first event of the trials, the 100-meter hurdles, Jackie won her heat. But Jodi Anderson scored more points with a better time. Patsy Walker won the shot put, never one of Jackie's strongest events. But all the athletes were shocked when Jane Frederick was unable to make the high jump because she had hurt her leg.

Jackie jumped six feet and then won the 200-meters to take the lead. But Cindy, Jodi, Patsy, and Jackie were so close together in points that any one of them could win the heptathlon. Only three of them could go on to the Olympics.

The next morning was Jackie's best event—the long jump. All of the women jumped well. Jodi Anderson jumped over 20 feet. But Jackie surprised them all. She flew down the runway, soared in the air, and landed at over 22 feet. She had set a new U.S. record.

Suddenly, Jackie was the talk of the competition. She could break Jane Frederick's U.S. record of 6,458 points. When Jane heard the talk, she went over to Jackie to encourage her. "Go for it," she said.

Jackie did. By the time the javelin and 800-meter events were finished, she set a new U.S. record of 6,520 points. Jackie, Jodi Anderson, and Cindy Greiner would represent the U.S. at the Olympics.

Now her Olympic moment had come. Jackie had qualified for the heptathlon and also for the long-jump competition. She would have a chance for two gold medals at the 1984 Olympics.

But was she ready? Two weeks before the Olympics she had pulled her hamstring muscle. She had to stop training so hard, rest, and spend time on physical therapy.

Jackie had heard a lot of talk about the women she would have to beat, women like Glynis Nunn of Australia. The reporters were writing that Glynis would win.

"I kept seeing her name in the paper," she said. "Bob told me not to worry about her, just to do the best I could and that would be enough. But I couldn't stop thinking about her."

By the end of the first day of the Olympic heptathlon, Jackie was in second place. One of her best events, the long jump, was first the next day. Each competitor would get three tries to do her best jump. But Jackie fouled her first two tries. She had to be careful on her third and last jump. She jumped over 20 feet, just enough to take the lead.

Jackie was tired. Her hamstring muscle hurt. But she still had to run the last event—the 800-meter race. Bob told her to stay close to Glynis, who would probably be the leader. If she could finish only 2.13 seconds behind her, Jackie could win the heptathlon.

Just across the track, Al Joyner was competing in the triple jump. No one had talked much about

Al. He was considered the third best jumper on the U.S. team and not given much of a chance to win. But after three tries out of six in jumping, Al was leading with a jump of over 57 feet.

Now the fourth round of jumping was beginning. Al looked across the track and saw Jackie getting ready for the 800-meter, a race in which the runners have to go twice around the track. Al left his event and ran over to where Jackie would have to pass him on the final turn of her track.

Glynis was leading the first time around. The second time, Jackie was trailing Glynis by almost 20 yards. Al started running alongside Jackie, but on the grass.

"Pump your arms, Jackie!" he yelled. "This is it!"

Jackie was a third of a second too slow. She lost the gold medal to Glynis by five points. The final score: Glynis Nunn 6,390, Jackie Joyner 6,385.

Al returned to the triple jump competition. No one was able to jump farther, and Al became the first U.S. athlete to win the triple jump in 80 years.

When he went over to the awards stand, Jackie had just received her silver medal. She stepped down and started to cry.

"It's okay," said Al.

"I'm not crying because I lost," she said. "I'm crying because you won. You fooled them all."

Jackie and Al became the first brother and sister to win Olympic medals in track and field on the same day. Al was to become famous for another reason besides his gold medal. When he

Jackie and Al celebrate their
medals in the 1984 Olympics.

went back to their hometown of East St. Louis,
Missouri, people would ask him, "Aren't you the
guy who cheered for his sister?"

Jackie refused to blame her loss on her hamstring. "It was my mentality," she said. "I doubted
my capabilities. I never thought in positive terms
about what it was going to take . . . to come
across the finish line first or to come across
doing my best."

She learned to focus on herself—what she
could do.

"Negative thoughts were filling her head,"
said Bob Kersee. "They turned gold to silver."

Jackie had learned early not to let negative
thoughts overcome her. It was a lesson she was
to remember again and again.

Jackie and Al in their hometown after the 1984
Olympics

SIDEBAR #9: NEEDING TO WIN

Hurdling

When Jackie and her friends used to jump over
bushes in East St. Louis, they didn't realize they
were practicing hurdling. But to win the heptathlon,
Jackie had to do more than jump.

Like sprinting, speed is important in hurdling.
But if a hurdler is tall, she has an advantage. Long
legs can help a hurdler clear the hurdle much
more easily.

A hurdler can't drag her foot or leg alongside
the hurdle or knock it over with her hand. The
hurdle has to be cleared smoothly. Hurdlers try
to get their front leg up with the knee almost

Jackie clearing a hurdle

straight. They bend their back leg as they jump. They lean forward over the hurdles. If they lean back, it slows them down.

Hurdlers have to be able to keep up a fast pace. They need good balance. They need to figure out how many steps they will need to take between hurdles. If they miss a step, they have to know how to make it up without losing speed. If they don't, hurdlers can fall and hurt themselves.

When some hurdlers first start jumping, they like to jump high. But they soon learn they lose time in the air. It's best to jump as close to the hurdle as possible and leave the high jumping for another event.

Chapter 6

A Coach for Life

After Glynis Nunn won the gold and Jackie came home with the silver medal, Bob said Jackie "learned to focus on what Jackie Joyner is doing. Not to underestimate others, but just get the job done and let the others come after her."

In the meantime, Jane Frederick recovered and took over the heptathlon record again. But not for long.

Jackie returned to UCLA and basketball, which she enjoyed playing. With her help the Bruins ended their season with a 20–10 record. She was the team's fourth best rebounder and sixth best career scorer. She was twice named most valuable player.

"If Jackie had specialized in basketball, she would have made the Olympic team," Coach Moore said.

But Bob had different ideas. At the time, athletic possibilities for women in basketball after college didn't exist. He thought Jackie would have many more opportunities if she worked on her track and field events. By that time, he had become Head Coach of the women's track team.

He and Jackie spent a lot of time training together. Their relationship had changed. It was more personal.

"We could talk about absolutely anything," said Jackie. "And whatever acclaim came to me didn't bother him." Some of the men she had dated had been upset that she was more famous than they were. Some of them couldn't handle her talent or her dedication.

Bob thought it was the first relationship of his life that might be for keeps. "I never had that many female friends," he said. "Who can when you're coaching from six o'clock in the morning until eight o'clock at night and watching video-tapes until ten and trying to go to sleep right after 'Nightline' goes off? One girlfriend I had told me, 'You put in more time with your athletics than you do with me.' I couldn't deny it."

Jackie listened to Bob more and more. She competed in as many indoor and outdoor track events for UCLA as she could. Her triple jump at over 43 feet was the best jump by an American woman in 1985. She ran the 400-meter hurdles in the fourth fastest time by an American woman and was the highest individual scorer in the NCAA outdoor championships in Austin, Texas that May.

Then she traveled to Europe for the summer to compete internationally in track and field. Carol Lewis, sister of athlete Carl Lewis, had set a new American indoor long jump record of nearly 22 feet in Japan. Jackie wanted to challenge that. In Zurich, Switzerland, she did—jumping for a new American outdoor record of 23' 9".

"That was as happy as I've ever seen her," said Al.

As soon as she came back, she went to Baton Rouge, Louisiana for the National Sports Festival at Southern University. Now called the Olympic Festival, it was an important stop on the way for any athlete who wanted to make the U.S. Olympic team. Her 3,942 points was a new U.S. first-day best, and she won all three events the second day too. She set a new NCAA record with 6,718 points although she still didn't break Jane Frederick's U.S. heptathlon record.

But Jane expected Jackie to do it soon. "I always thought she would be the one to lead the next generation, and it had to do with the kind of person she was. She had a sense of purpose. With Kersee's direction, she really gave herself to all seven events."

Meanwhile, Jackie and Bob's relationship was becoming more serious. One evening Bob asked Jackie to meet him at the beach. They talked about her scores for the next NCAA heptathlon. Nothing more was said. But when Jackie came home that night, she thought Bob was beginning to have feelings that were more than a coach had for his athlete.

"Nothing came of it at the time, but I went home and looked in the mirror and said, 'I think he likes me.'"

Bob and Jackie began to date. They didn't want anyone else to know they were dating because they were afraid other athletes would think that Bob was helping Jackie more than the others in training. Jackie was sharing a house with teammate Valerie Brisco, so she told Valerie. But Valerie didn't believe her.

Bob realized he had finally found someone he could share his life with on and off the track.

"What was wrong with me was trying to find a wife outside athletics and trying to convince her that this is a big part of my life and not to get mad because I come home and have four or five athletes with me and ask what's to eat for all of us."

At the same time, the couple worried about what it might do to their working relationship.

"Bobby was a great person and a great friend," said Jackie, "but when we thought about love, we also had to think about what we might lose. We were afraid that if it didn't work out together, it might jeopardize our wonderful relationship as friends. And we didn't want that to happen."

Finally, Bob took a chance. In Houston, in the summer of 1985 they went to a baseball game at the Astrodome. Between pitches, Bob talked about marriage. It took Jackie a while to catch on.

Bob and Jackie enjoyed being together and decided to get married.

She thought he was talking about marriage in general. At last he said, "You know, we get along so well, we might as well get married."

55

Six months later, on January 11, 1986, they were married. The wedding took place at Saint Luke's Baptist Church in Long Beach, California. Bob was Associate Pastor of the church.

Jackie's brother Al had one of the biggest roles. He gave the bride away and made sure the photographs were taken. In fact, he did both at the same time.

"When they asked 'Who gives this woman?' I was out in the crowd showing Jeannette Bolden [a member of the 1984 U.S. Olympic gold medal relay team] how to work the camera. I said, 'Agh! I do! And good luck,'" said Al.

The bride and groom laughed as each tried to put a wedding ring on the other's hand. "This is going to be a happy marriage," said the minister.

Afterward, Bob and Jackie flew to East St. Louis. Jackie wanted Bob to meet the rest of her family and see where she had grown up. Then they went back to California, sports, and married life.

In 1989, Bob talked about their marriage, saying, "We want to make it in terms of what we've got to do athletically, and we want to stay married for the rest of our lives. So we've got rules in terms of our coach-athlete relationship and our husband-wife relationship. Jackie is easy to coach, but she's opinionated, and I'm opinionated. I'm a yeller; I'm going to get my point across. I've been married 2½ years; I've been coaching for 17. So I know more about coaching than about being married. Jackie's an athlete of mine, and I'm not going to treat her any better or any worse than I treat any of my athletes."

Once a reporter asked Bob if Jackie had any bad traits.

"She's hard-headed," Bob said.

"I am not," Jackie said.

"See what I mean?" Bob said.

Jackie admits she is difficult to coach. She always wants to be better so she drives herself hard.

" . . . when Bob tells me to take a day off, I'm likely to work out anyway. That's hard on a coach. Here you've got an athlete who should rest, and this athlete wants to do more and more. I just have to realize that when he says rest, I should rest."

Sometimes they don't agree about what Jackie should do. Once, at a meet, Bob suggested that Jackie enter the 200-meter race for practice. Jackie said no, and they argued. She spent the rest of the time angry and walking around until the meet was over and Bob could drive her home.

Jackie says: "I am a bit stubborn. I guess I ought to be the one who says 'I'm sorry, you were right.' But it's hard for me to say that . . . . But at least we keep it on the athletic field. When we go home, it's as husband and wife. That means Bobby laying on the couch, asking me if I'll run him some bath water."

One of the reasons their off-the-track, on-the-track relationship works so well is because of teamwork. They help each other. For example, Jackie hates to cook, so Bob took over the cooking.

At the same time, Jackie says: " . . . he likes to be catered to, just like he caters to us out on the field. So I turn around and do the little things he needs to have done."

Because of the demands of sports and her private life, Jackie still had to finish a half year of school to get her degree. She took off the 1985–1986 year, planning to return the following school year to finish up.

But Jackie didn't plan to spend the year resting. Instead, she started another round of sports competitions and was about to go on to new triumphs.

SIDEBAR #10: OLYMPIC MEN

Jesse Owens: The Sidewalk Champion

When Jesse Owens was in fifth grade, he was asked to try out for the track team. Jesse explained that he had jobs after school and couldn't practice with the team. The coach arranged for him to practice every morning before school began. They would meet at a sidewalk near the school. When Jesse broke his first record six months later, his coach called him "the sidewalk champion."

Jesse had to fight illness, poverty, and prejudice all his life. Youngest in a family of ten children, he had pneumonia and other illnesses. His parents were former slaves. It was hard for them to make a living. But Jesse's mother, Mary, insisted he go to high school instead of to work. Jesse became

Jesse Owens easily won the gold in Berlin, 1936.

captain of the track team and student body president in a high school that was mostly white.

In 1936, after breaking records at Ohio State University, Jesse went to Berlin for the Olympics.

Adolph Hitler, the German Nazi dictator, had said that the Olympics would show that blonde, blue-eyed athletes were better than any others. By the time Jesse had won his third gold medal, Hitler had disappeared from the stadium to avoid shaking Jesse's hand.

Fifteen years later, Jesse returned to Germany for a visit. By that time, Hitler was dead, and the Nazis had lost World War II. Jesse was invited to appear at the Olympic stadium. When he ran around the track, 75,000 people cheered him. When Jesse ran over to the mayor of Berlin, the mayor stood up, held out both hands, and said, "Fifteen years ago, Hitler would not shake your hand. Here, I give you both of mine." And he threw his arms around Jesse and hugged him.

Chapter 7

Smashing Records

Jackie had joined Bob's World Class Track Club in 1986 and was now competing for it rather than for UCLA. Bob had formed the club because so many athletes he had worked with had graduated from college but still wanted to work with him. The club scheduled appearances at meets for the athletes. Bob's club, like many others, received money from sponsors. Adidas and International Chemical Industries helped pay for the athletes' training.

Adidas also sponsored some individual athletes like Jackie. In return for using her name and photo to advertise its clothing and shoes, they gave Jackie a monthly living allowance and paid her travel expenses. Jackie began appearing on TV and at special events around the country. She was becoming a star.

She soon showed everyone her star power. Her first heptathlon competition of the season was at the Mount San Antonio College Relays in

California in April. It was a small meet. Few people stayed for the second day's competition. No one expected that Jackie would break Jane Frederick's record there. But she did, scoring a personal best of 6,910 points.

The only problem was that it wasn't official. During the 200-meter race, the automatic timer had broken. Jackie's score could not be put down in the record books. But everyone who heard about the results knew she was on her way to making history in the heptathlon.

Rain and cold greeted her in May in Austria at the Goetzis International, a world-famous track and field meet. Bad weather couldn't stop Jackie. She scored 6,841 and finally officially broke Jane Frederick's record.

Honors, like the NCAA awarding her the Broderick Cup for the second year in a row as the best female collegiate athlete, were coming in. Jackie, while happy to receive the awards, was more focused on the upcoming Goodwill Games in Moscow in July.

The Games were the idea of Ted Turner, the communications executive who had started television's Cable News Network (CNN) in Atlanta, Georgia. He thought that because the U.S. had not sent athletes to the Summer Olympics in Moscow in 1980 and because the Soviet Union had, in turn, not sent theirs to the 1984 Olympics in Los Angeles, both countries had missed out on an exciting competition.

Ted Turner decided to bring athletes from the West (the U.S., Canada, and European countries) together with those from the East (the Soviet Union, Cuba, and East Germany) in a giant track meet. The games would be shown worldwide on one of Ted Turner's television networks.

Jackie was excited about appearing on TV. But she was more interested in setting a new world record. Sportswriters and coaches had long argued whether a woman could ever score 7,000 in a heptathlon. Most thought it couldn't be done.

On July 7, 1986, Jackie stepped on the field filled with her three D's: determination, dedication and desire.

First, she set an American best in the 100-meter high hurdles. Next came two personal bests: one in the high jump of six feet, two inches, and one in the 200-meter. With 4,151 points, Jackie had beaten the first-day world-best record that had been set in 1985.

Everyone now knew that Jackie was determined to set a new world record. She wanted to score 7,000 points. They still thought it could never be done.

Sometimes athletes slow down after a good first day. Jackie still had three more events to go. Maybe, thought the other competitors, they might have a chance.

It was not to be. In her favorite event, the long jump, Jackie leaped a world-record-shattering 23

Jackie's amazing long jump at the Goodwill Games, Moscow, 1986

feet. She threw the javelin over 163 feet—her best throw ever.

Finally, only the 800-meter race was left. Jackie knew she had won the gold medal. But she still wanted to score over 7,000 points. She couldn't relax. All her efforts went into thinking and planning the race.

The Goodwill Games announcer told the crowd that Jackie needed to run the race in under two minutes and 25 seconds to break 7,000 points. As Jackie ran, the crowd of 25,000 cheered her on. By now, everyone was on her side.

Jackie finished in 2:10.02! Her score: 7,148 points, 202 points better than the old world record. Jackie's closest competitor in the games, Sabine Paetz, an East German and the former world record holder, came running out to congratulate her. The crowd stood and cheered. And the announcer, speaking in English and Russian, couldn't stop saying, "It's marvelous. It's magnificent."

Jackie had become the first American woman to hold the world record in a multievent since Babe Didrikson Zaharias's record-setting triathlon (100-yard dash, high jump, and javelin throw) more than 50 years earlier.

It would have been easy for Jackie to say "I told you so" to the reporters who interviewed her after her win. Instead, she said:

"I feel very blessed today to come here and do this. I feel that I've paid my dues. I knew good things would come my way because I have been very humble and patient waiting for this to happen."

But Dwight Stones, a high jumper who was now a TV commentator, just couldn't accept what Jackie had done.

"No way you're ever going to do that again," he said to her.

A month later, she proved him wrong. In August, she competed at the U.S. Olympic Sports Festival in Houston, Texas. The temperature was over 100 degrees Fahrenheit—not the best kind of weather for any sports activity, let alone a heptathlon.

After the first day's events, Jackie gave a press conference sitting on bags of ice. It would have been easy to do less than her best in such terrible heat. She already had set the world record.

But Jackie's brother Al, her old coach Nino Fennoy, and her father came to see her. She gave them quite a show. Not only did she break 7,000 again, she broke her own record by scoring 7,158 points.

Even Bob was surprised and impressed. "To do it again in this short period of time is truly amazing," he said.

"I had my doubts I would make it coming around the quarter in the 800," Jackie said, "but all the time I was running, I kept remembering what Bobby says in the morning when I'm doing my roadwork. He says, 'Go to your arms. Start pumping.' As soon as I did, I started to relax."

Now the awards came pouring in. In 1987, she was given the Jesse Owens Memorial Award, named for the famous Olympic track star. *Track & Field* magazine honored her as Women's Athlete of the Year. The U.S. Olympic Committee decided she was Sportswoman of the Year. She became only the eighth woman in 67 years to win the Sullivan Award, which is given by the Amateur Athletics Union to the nation's outstanding amateur athlete. Jackie had to compete with U.S. Naval Academy basketball star David Robinson and University of Miami football quarterback Vinny Testaverde.

Al Joyner couldn't get over it.

"She beat out a Heisman Trophy [a major award in football] winner. That's something I can tell my grandchildren about. She wasn't just the best woman athlete in America. They voted her the best American athlete, period."

While Jackie enjoyed all the awards, she thought her most memorable moment was setting the world record in Houston. After competing in other countries, Jackie wanted to perform for Americans.

"I went to Houston to put on a performance for the American people after setting the world heptathlon record at the Goodwill Games in Moscow," she said.

She was happy that so many people were in the stands in Houston to watch her.

"I've worked so hard to put the multievents on the map, as far as Americans are concerned," she said. "Now people are finally involved. It's a good feeling that people are coming around."

Even though she had become a world-famous athlete, Jackie still had to finish school to get her degree. So, in December, she went back to UCLA and graduated with a major in history. She and Bob bought a house in Long Beach, California, and they traveled daily to UCLA so that Bob could coach the women's track team and Jackie could continue her training.

Now it was time for them to focus on the Olympics in Seoul, Korea, only a year away.

SIDEBAR #11: WOMEN AND THE OLYMPICS

When the Greeks began the Olympic Games, they wouldn't let women compete. Women weren't even allowed to watch the games.

Later, the women started their own Olympics. They were held one month before the regular Olympics and called the Heraean Games in honor of the Greek goddess Hera, who ruled over women and the earth. Only the young and unmarried were allowed to compete. They raced barefoot or in sandals. The winners were given olive branches and a share of the cow sacrificed to Hera.

Pierre de Coubertin, the founder of the modern Olympics, agreed with the Greeks that women should not compete. He thought the most important thing a woman could do at the Olympics was to crown the winner. He was not alone in his beliefs.

For centuries, women did not participate in

sports. Some people believed that women were not supposed to work so hard. Others thought that women should be helpless. Many were shocked at the idea of women wearing little clothing and showing their bare arms and legs.

In 1896, when the first modern Olympics was held in Athens, Melpomene, a Greek woman, asked to compete in the marathon. The officials said no.

Melpomene decided to run anyway. She got ready out of sight of the officials and ran so they could not see her among the men. The men ran from Marathon to Athens, through the hot, dusty countryside. Many stopped for water, brandy or wine. Many dropped out. Melpomene lost sight of the men, but kept on running. People stared and made fun of her. She passed tired runners lying in the shade, who were surprised to see her.

At nearly three hours after the start of the race, the Greek champion, Spiridon Louis, came into the stadium. The audience cheered and threw flowers, hats, jewels, and money at him. Nearly one and a half hours later, Melpomene reached the stadium. She was not allowed to enter, so she ran the final lap outside the stadium.

Women were first allowed to be in the Olympics in 1900—although out of 1,077 people competing, only 11 were women. In 1920, female swimmers were the first women from the U.S. to gain full Olympic status.

Long after slavery was done away with in the U.S., African-American women still were not allowed to compete in the Olympics. White sporting organizations kept them out. In 1895, some black colleges began organizing tennis matches and tournaments for their students. Later, community groups, some women's athletic clubs, and colleges started programs for African-American women in basketball, swimming, tennis, and track. But it was not until 1932 that the first African-American women—Tydie Pickett and Louise Stokes—were chosen to participate in the Olympics in Los Angeles.

Prejudice against women in the Olympics still continues. It wasn't until 1960 that women were allowed to run long-distance races. It was thought to be too hard for women.

In 1984, women ran their first Olympic

Alice Coachman (middle) won a gold medal for the USA in 1948.

marathon, the long-distance race that is the symbol of the ancient games. Five sports, including weight-lifting and wrestling, are still open only to men. According to one Olympic official, women will never be allowed to compete in weight-lifting because "women are not supposed to grunt onstage."

Joan Benoit won the marathon at the 1984 Olympics in Los Angeles.

Nawal el Moutawakil of Morocco after winning the gold in 1984 for the 400-meter hurdle race

In the 1992 Olympics, the US women's basketball team played against the Russian team.

Chapter 8

Photo Finish

Jackie had scored 7,158, but she wasn't satisfied. She wanted to see how far she could go. Now she was aiming at 7,200 in the heptathlon.

Before she could compete in the Olympics, however, she had to practice, train, and enter as many events as she could. It was important to compete in as many heptathlons as possible. Jackie could get more practice that way, size up the competition, and try to set her own records.

First came the Mobil Indoor Track and Field Grand Prix. Athletes compete in a series of races during the season. At the end, their points are added up for an overall score. Jackie won the women's title and was named the meet's Outstanding Athlete.

Next was the Pepsi Invitational in May 1987. Jackie set records in the long jump of 22 feet, 7 inches and in the 100-meter hurdles at 12.6 seconds. Her 100-meter time would have smashed the American record of 12.79, but, again, a timer had broken. Her record was not official. The only event she still had trouble with was the javelin. Each time, the javelin throw would lower her score.

At the national outdoor championships in San Jose in California in June, Jackie tried for another world record. She almost made it.

She long-jumped 23' 9½", half an inch better than her U.S. heptathlon best and the longest jump ever by a U.S. female athlete in a heptathlon. But, again, it didn't count. Official rules say that athletes can't be helped by wind when setting records. Any wind more than 4.4 miles an hour is thought to be too strong. The wind was clocked at five miles an hour during Jackie's jump.

Then her old problem with the javelin occurred. Jackie had two fouls. Her throws landed outside the boundary. If she didn't throw well the next time, she might lose the chance to be one of the top three finishers and go on to the important world championships in Rome.

Jackie threw a tame 130', and finished up strongly in the 800-meters. Her final score was 6,979—the third highest total of all time.

Bob understood that Jackie was disappointed, but he told her: "You have to realize you're chasing your own goals. How can you get down on yourself because you're not up to your own standards?"

Jackie kept on practicing the javelin. Bob wanted her to practice and rest, but Jackie wanted to go to the Pan Am Games in Indianapolis—just two weeks before the world championships.

Jackie throwing the javelin

Bob was against it, but Jackie insisted on going. It was good luck for them that they did. A fan came up to Jackie in Indianapolis and asked her to sign a photograph in a magazine. Jackie started to sign her name and then took another look at the photo. Next to her picture was one of Heike Drechsler, East Germany's leading long jumper. With a jump of 24' 5½", Heike held the world's record.

But what made Jackie stop and stare was the way Heike was jumping in the picture. She had jumped with her legs straight out in front of her. Bob had asked Jackie to try jumping that way, but Jackie hadn't done it yet.

She decided to try it a few days later on her sixth jump in the long-jump competition at the Pan Am Games. As she soared off the take-off board, she put both legs out in front of her. It worked! Jackie tied Heike's record and was now the first woman to hold world records in a single event and a multievent at the same time.

No one was happier than Bob. He dropped to his knees and started crying. He couldn't stop. Reporters asked him why.

"I'm so emotional because we were so close to not coming here. I have to ask myself: Am I so over-protective that I could have kept her from this?"

Jackie went over and hugged Bob. She even joked with him and teased, saying: "So now I can long-jump, huh?"

It was the perfect set-up for Jackie to begin the world championships—feeling good about herself and her abilities. Even though the weather was hot and humid in Rome, Jackie started well. She got the highest first day total in history—4,256 points—and 105 points better than any of her other scores.

But on the second day, the javelin did her in again. Her throw was 149' 10", not one of her better efforts. Before the 800-meter race, the last event, started, she was ahead by 60 points but had a bad headache and started to feel dehydrated. Dehydration happens when athletes sweat in the heat and don't drink enough water to replace what their bodies have lost. It can cause people to feel faint, dizzy, or sick.

"I drank some water and hoped not to die," said Jackie. Then she started to race. She ended up with 2:16.29 and missed her world record by 30 points. Still, she won the games with the title of world champion in the heptathlon. Her score, 7,128, was the third best in history and way ahead of second-place Larisa Nikitina of the Soviet Union with 6,564 and Jackie's old friend Jane Frederick of the U.S., who scored 6,502.

Then it was on to face the woman who held the world record in the long jump with her— Heike Drechsler.

" . . . You know they'll force the best out of each other," said Bob about the two women.

Heike and Jackie after the long-jump event in Rome, 1988

"And no matter who wins, you know it won't change their feelings for each other."

In fact, while competing against each other both women had become friends. There was great rivalry between the U.S. and the East German athletes in the 1980s. Sometimes, the East Germans would hide Jackie's marker when she was ready for the long jump. Someone might walk into her path as she got set for the shot put. Heike Drechsler, however, told her teammates to stop it.

Jackie didn't get mad at the East Germans; she just decided to win.

"I have a lot of respect for a lot of people," she said. "But don't walk over me, and don't do something bad to me because I'll change that."

Off the field, she and Heike had friendly talks about their private lives; on the field, Jackie got ready to beat her.

Jackie started off strong with a jump of 23' 4½". But she knew she would have to do better than that. On her third jump, she made it, reaching nearly a foot farther with 24' 1¾".

What Jackie didn't know was that Heike was not able to jump her best. She had hurt her knee and was in great pain. Her knee hurt so badly that Heike passed on her last two jumps. The gold medal was Jackie's.

Jackie was sorry for Heike but knew what it was like to be injured. They hugged each other; then Jackie and Bob celebrated.

There was even more to celebrate. Jackie's brother Al had gotten engaged to Florence Griffith. Florence was a teammate of Jackie's at UCLA. After she graduated, she stayed to work with Bob. Al was training with Bob, also, and the two met at UCLA.

Florence had won a silver medal at the Olympics in 1984 in the 200-meter dash. She also won the silver in the dash at the world championships and a gold medal as a member of the women's 4 × 100 relay. To let the world know they were engaged, she gave the gold medal to Al.

The press started calling all of them "The First Family of Track."

Again, awards for Jackie poured in. But Jackie went back to Los Angeles and a new job. She became a part-time assistant coach with the UCLA women's basketball team.

Coach Moore was more than happy with Jackie's help.

"She thoroughly enjoys everything she's doing," the coach said. "She makes everything feel special. That's her natural way. She could be carrying the heaviest burden in the world, and she'd still be smiling."

Jackie also remained quiet and modest. The press compared her to Florence Griffith, who liked to race wearing lace stretch suits and paint her fingernails different colors. When she was asked why she didn't wear the same kind of clothes that Florence did, Jackie said:

"Oh, it's nice, but it's not me. I couldn't concentrate on what I was doing . . . I was brought up to wear long dresses. Never to be flashy. My mother used to dress me from the fifties when I was a teenager. She was only a child herself, raising a child, and she wanted to protect me. . . . "

Jackie didn't like to make a fuss. "If you didn't know her," said her friend Greg Foster, the world high hurdles champion, "you'd never guess she's the greatest female athlete in the world."

SIDEBAR #12: NEEDING TO WIN

The Shot Put and the Javelin

Imagine lifting a solid ball of metal. It is almost nine pounds—about the weight of seven heavy

Throwing the shot

schoolbooks. Now imagine throwing those books all at once as far as you can. That's what Jackie and the other athletes who compete in the shot put need to do.

Jackie can't throw the shot. She has to push it. She is not allowed to run to get up speed or strength. Instead, she has to stand still inside a 7-foot-wide circle. If she moves outside that circle, it is a foul. The hand she uses for putting the shot can't drop until she is finished, otherwise that is a foul too.

The javelin is much lighter. Women's javelins weigh one pound, five ounces, and are 7' ½" long. Unlike the shot put, javelin throwers can get up speed by running before they throw. The throw is very important. It has to be overhand, and the

Throwing the javelin

javelin has to come down point first. Otherwise, the throw is no good.

Most people can imagine throwing the javelin. But, again, it is more tricky than it looks. Good javelin athletes can throw a long way. One of Jackie's best javelin throws was over 164'—as long as the height of 27 tall men put together.

Babe Didrikson throwing the javelin

SIDEBAR #13: OLYMPIC WOMEN

Flo-Jo: Running After Jackrabbits

Florence Griffith-Joyner grew up with her mother and ten brothers and sisters in Watts, California. But she often visited her father who lived in the Mojave Desert. There, Florence got early sprint training chasing after jackrabbits, one of the fastest animals on earth.

Florence liked being different. She changed hairstyles often, fixing her hair herself. She got a boa constrictor snake as a pet and left the house with it wrapped around her neck.

The U.S. Olympic team officials were not happy about Florence being different at the 1984 Olympics. She liked to wear bright, glowing body suits. She had six-inch fingernails. The officials said they wouldn't give her a spot on the sprint-relay team unless she cut her nails. They said her nails were too long for Florence to be able to pass

Al Joyner and Florence Griffith Joyner after she won a gold medal in Seoul, Korea

the baton smoothly during the race. Florence said no. The relay team ran and won without her.

Florence did win the silver in the 200-meter dash. Then she dropped out of racing. She took a job with a big company.

In 1986, she got back into competition. Her husband, Al Joyner, Jackie's brother, became her coach. At the Olympic trials, nobody expected much from the girl from Watts. On the day of the qualifying heats, Florence turned up in a bright green track suit with one leg cut out. Gwen Torrence, one of the U.S. runners, said, "If you're going to wear outfits like that, you'd better do something in them."

After the heats were over, Florence had smashed nearly every world record. Florence died in 1998, but memories of her grace live on.

Chapter 9

Trials and Triumphs

Jackie and Bob decided to dedicate all of their wins in 1988 to "two people who aren't here: our mothers." They decided they would try to enjoy everything.

In February, she set a long-jump record at the Vitalis/U.S. Olympic Invitational. In Fairfax, Virginia, she broke another record in the 60-meter high hurdles.

Jackie and Gail Devers, the Olympic racer, competed with each other all spring to see who would set the American 100-meter hurdles record. First, Gail hit 12.71 seconds; then Jackie turned in a time of 12.70. Gail pushed it to 12.61, and a week later, Jackie tied her.

But while Jackie was busy setting records, she and Bob also worried about her asthma. Jackie still had attacks and hated to admit it.

"I control so much of what I do, and I can't control this asthma. Sometimes I don't want to accept that I have asthma . . . . I can't handle an attack. I panic," she said.

Once, that winter, Bob found her bent over, trying to get air into her lungs. She couldn't stop coughing. He and Al tried to persuade her to go to the hospital. Jackie didn't want to go, but they finally took her in the car to the emergency room. Then, she didn't want to go in because she was sure she had it under control.

Bob decided not to listen to her or argue with her.

"I just picked her up and carried her through the door," he said.

Jackie ended up spending two days in the hospital.

They had another scare when Jackie fell in the last indoor meet of the season. In the 55-meter hurdles at the Mobil/USA Indoor Track and Field Championships, Jackie slipped when she started. She hit one hurdle with her knee, another with her foot, and ended up on her face, sliding onto the track.

Every athlete worries about an accident like this. One mistake or slip can be very important. A broken leg or ankle would have caused her to sit out the Olympic trials and miss the Olympics. A more serious injury could have ended her career in sports.

Luckily, Jackie wasn't hurt. She even said that if she had been playing baseball, she would have scored a run.

The First Family of Track and Field roared into Indianapolis for the Olympic trials in July. Florence put on a great performance. She set a new world record in the 100-meter dash and won the 200-meter race, just short of a new world record.

Of course, reporters talked not only about Florence as an athlete but about what she looked like and what she wore. She had decided to turn up in one-legged body suits. One day, she wore a bright green one; the next was purple. The media started calling her Flo-Jo, taken from her first name and her married last name.

Reporters asked Jackie if she was jealous of all the attention Flo-Jo was getting.

"We're not competitive," she said. "The media try to make it look that way because we're family. I think Florence's . . . appearance was very good for our sport. It attracted many viewers who otherwise might not have watched track and field."

Then it was Jackie's turn. It was 103 degrees the first day of the heptathlon. But it didn't matter to Jackie. She set three heptathlon U.S. records: the 100-meter hurdles, the 200-meter sprint, and the high jump.

There was a sudden rainstorm. It didn't matter to Jackie. She threw her second-best shot put ever and ended the day with 4,367 points. On the second day, Jackie moved ahead of Cindy Greiner, the second-place finisher, by nearly 1,000 points. Jackie's final score was 7,215.

"Jackie does her thing, and the rest of us compete for runner-up," said Cindy.

Suffering from the heat, Jackie lay down on a

training table filled with bags of ice to talk to reporters. While she was talking, she heard the announcer name the athletes who had made the 1988 U.S. Olympic Triple-Jump Team.

Jackie knew that Al was competing while she finished her 800-meter run. Now she stopped talking and listened for Al's name.

But Al's was not one of the three names announced for the team.

Jackie put her head down on the table and cried. She couldn't seem to stop crying.

Later, Al said, "She cried when I won in Los Angeles, and now she's cried when I lost."

But Al was on the plane when the Track and Field team traveled to the 1988 Olympics in Seoul, Korea.

"I've got to go now," he said. "I got my gold medal in 1984, but my sister and my wife got silvers. I've got to help them get golds."

As always, the First Family of Track and Field worked together for each other. When Flo-Jo left Bob's World Class Runners club to train with Al, Bob had said, "She was free to do what she thought best. We [will] not let gold medals and endorsements interfere with the family."

But perhaps Jackie put it best: "Remember, no matter what we say, we all love each other."

Now the pressure was on Jackie. She had shown the world that a woman athlete could score over 7,000 points in the heptathlon. She had shown that, not once but three times. Now she had to prove it again to the world at the Olympics. She also wanted the long jump world record back. She had lost it in June when Galina Chistyakova of the Soviet Union had jumped 24' 8¼". Of course, her old friend and rival, Heike Drechsler of East Germany, would be there, too.

The plane ride to Seoul was 12 hours long, but Jackie was too excited to sleep. She was looking forward to the competition and determined that this time she would bring home the gold.

As usual, nothing came that easily for Jackie. From the first day she had problems. She won the hurdles but twisted her knee in the second event, the high jump. She was in pain, but she went on. She tried to forget her pain, and she was able to get a good shot put score. By the end of the day, she had won the 200-meter race, and she was in first place.

The next day, still with a sore and aching knee, she set a record long jump. When she finished the heptathlon with an 800-meter race time of 2.08.51 minutes, she had set a new world heptathlon record: 7,291 points. Jackie had won the gold at last!

Jackie heard the band play the national anthem, "The Star-Spangled Banner," as she stood on the victory stand. As she felt her new gold medal around her neck, she thought of her mother: "I always assumed she would be with me to see this," she said.

The long-jump contest was still ahead. Jackie competed against Galina Chistyakova, the world record holder, and Heike Drechsler five days after her heptathlon win.

First, Galina took the lead with a jump of 23' 4". Then Heike beat her with a leap of 23' 8¼". It seemed the best Jackie could do was to win the silver with a jump of 23' 6". She had fouled on two of her tries.

Now it was the fifth round. Jackie had only two jumps left. All of a sudden, she ran down the runway and sailed into the air with a jump of 24' 3½". Jackie had become the first American woman to win the gold medal in the Olympic long jump and the first American woman to win a field event since 1956, when Mildred McDaniel won the high jump.

The First Family of Track and Field continued to mop up the medals. Along with Jackie's two gold ones, Flo-Jo won three—one for the 100-meter run, one for the 200-meter race, and a third with 4 2 100 relay team.

No longer would officials say that Florence's nails were too long to pass the baton. An Olympic photo shows her holding her medals with her six-inch nails—each one painted with a shiny color or glitter.

Almost everyone was happy for Jackie and Flo-Jo. Many people had long respected Jackie as an athlete and as a person.

"I don't know a person in this world who has a negative thing to say about Jackie," said Fred Thompson, an assistant coach for the 1988

Jackie lands after her record-breaking long jump.

American Olympic team. "She's a lady. And it's not just on her lips—she goes out there and does things."

But those who were jealous of Jackie and Flo-Jo tried to make trouble. First, Canadian sprinter Ben Johnson set a world record of 9.79 in the 100-meter dash.

"This world record will last fifty years, maybe one hundred," Johnson said. "More important than the world record was to beat Carl Lewis and win the gold." Carl Lewis, a sprinter and long jumper, had won four gold medals in 1984 and two in Seoul.

Just a few days later, the medal was taken from Johnson and given to Lewis. Johnson had been found to have used a performance-enhancing steroid drug. Steroids and many other drugs are strictly forbidden for use in the Olympics.

Ben Johnson was not the only one. Ten other athletes were stripped of their medals after their tests showed they had used drugs.

Bob and Jackie celebrating her wins

Some athletes took them in the hopes that they would be able to do better than they usually did. Some athletes did not know they had been given steroids. A few years later, a few East German coaches said they had slipped steroids into the meals of their swimmers. The swimmers never knew.

Flo-Jo and Jackie in 1988

Jackie and Flo-Jo knew they were clean. Neither had ever taken drugs. In fact, Jackie did not even take her asthma medicine because it had some drugs that were not allowed by Olympic rules.

Yet, Joaquim Cruz of Brazil, another Olympic athlete, suddenly said he knew that Jackie and Flo-Jo took anabolic steroids.

His reason for saying this was that he thought Flo-Jo's looks had changed over the years.

"Florence, in 1984, you could see an extremely feminine person, but today she looks more like a man than a woman . . . So these people must be doing something which isn't normal to gain all these muscles," he said.

The Olympic Committee said Cruz's statement was nonsense. All of Jackie's and Flo-Jo's tests were free of drugs.

"I'm sad and sorry that people are implying that I'm doing something because I've worked hard to get where I am today," Jackie said. "There are a lot of reasons now why I won't even take a drink. I don't feel like putting anything into my body. It took a long time before I would even take an aspirin."

Cruz later said that he never made such a statement. He backed down, and everyone forgot he had said Jackie and Flo-Jo were on steroids.

There was nothing but praise for Jackie. Jackie could have rested and enjoyed her fame. But she was already involved in doing something for others, in giving something to those she had left behind in East St. Louis. So she left her gold medals at home and started traveling back to the future.

SIDEBAR #14: WHAT ARE STEROIDS?

Steroids are dangerous drugs that may help athletes train harder by changing their bodies. Women who take steroids, for example, develop bodies that are harder and have more muscles—like men. Men who take steroids are able to develop more strength and more muscles.

But steroids also can do terrible things to people. People on steroids may get very angry for no reason. They can be violent and hurt others. They have less control over themselves and what they do.

Steroids may cause cancer. They can also hurt the liver and other organs of the body.

The Olympic Committee tests athletes at random all during the games. No one knows who will be tested at any time.

Most Olympic athletes do not want to compete against anyone on drugs, nor do they want to take drugs themselves. Most have spent too much time training and working hard for this big event to lose out.

"I want a clean sport," said runner Mary Decker Slaney at the 1988 games when Johnson was stripped of his medal and suspended for two years. "The fact that a thing this big can't be swept under the rug is a sign of hope."

Kristin Otto, an East German swimmer who won six golds in 1988, said (when she learned about the coaches who might have put steroids in her food), "It is important to research what really happened, to ask officials what they did. I passed every drug test, but I can't be sure what was put into my drinks and food."

SIDEBAR #15: HIGHLIGHTS OF THE 1988 SUMMER OLYMPICS: SEOUL

The opening of the 1988 games in Seoul was important for all Koreans. Crowds rose and cheered as a seventy-six-year-old man, Sohn Kee-Chung, ran into the stadium carrying the Olympic torch. Fifty-two years before, Japan ruled Korea. Sohn Kee-Chung had been forced to compete under a Japanese name, Kitei Son, and a Japanese flag. Now his country was showing the world that Kitei Son's gold medal really belonged to Korea. Other highlights:

• After 64 years, tennis became an Olympic sport again. West German Steffi Graf won the women's singles; Miloslav Mecir of Czechoslovakia won the men's.

• Table tennis, or Ping Pong, became a new Olympic sport. All the women's medals were won

Sohn Kee-Chung at the 1988 Olympics in Seoul, Korea

by the Chinese; first and second place in the men's went to Korea.

• Daniela Silvas of Romania won three gold medals, two silvers, and a bronze in gymnastics.

• Two athletes from Kenya, Paul Ereng in the 800-meters and Peter Rono in the 1500-meters, won the gold in the middle-distance events. In the 800-meters, Paul ran with his countryman, Nixon Kiprotich. They had a plan. Nixon ran very fast to tire out the other fast runners. Then Paul was able to come from behind and win.

• American Matt Biondi swam and came up with five gold medals, a silver, and a bronze.

• The Soviet Union won the most gold medals with 55. The East Germans were second with 37. For the first time in 12 years, all the leading Olympic nations, except Cuba and Ethiopia, took part in the games.

Chapter 10

New Gold, New Goals

"One's heart should always be geared toward making someone else's life better," said Jackie. "Where I come from, it was a struggle for me. The young people back there don't think there is a way out, and I want them to know that there is a way out . . . . "

After bringing home the gold, Jackie turned toward her new goal—starting the Jackie Joyner-Kersee Community Foundation to help inner-city youth. She decided that one of the best ways to help them with sports, cultural, and educational programs was to raise money for a new recreation center. Jackie remembered all the fun she had and everything she learned at the Mary E. Brown Community Center in East St. Louis. Sadly, that center had closed because there was no money to keep it open.

Jackie tried to raise money by making appearances, speaking to groups, and endorsing products. Before the Olympics, Jackie had a hard time getting sponsors. Many companies were not interested in an African-American woman athlete.

After she won the gold, however, three big companies signed her up, and two more continued to work with her. Jackie made sure that part of all the money she got went to her foundation. She wanted to make East St. Louis a better place to live.

"East St. Louis has been called a bad place," Jackie said. "But I feel that there are a lot of people here who care about human beings being human. All we need to do is to get together, and we can become a great city.

"I'm proud to be from East St. Louis, and I don't hide it. Some might be ashamed, but where you come from and what you are now go hand in hand."

"She came from a city without hope," Bob said. "And yet when you talk to her, it's like there's all the hope in the world."

Along with developing the community center, Jackie wanted to make sure there was money to send young athletes from East St. Louis and other poor places to the Junior Olympics.

"There were people, when I was little, reaching into their pockets trying to make sure I could go to the Junior Olympics, trying to make things possible for me. I feel that in return I can do that for the next generation. . . . I hope I can inspire someone to take the right path and be successful," she said.

Beside helping children, she knew how to show them a good time and another life. In November, 1988, she and Bob took 100 children from East St. Louis to New York City for the yearly Macy's Thanksgiving Day Parade. The children saw balloons, floats, dancers, and clowns. Most of them had never left home before. They also saw a new, exciting life they could aim for.

There was more work to be done and more money to be raised. Jackie hit the road. She spoke to children in schools, hospitals, and churches all over the country. But no matter where she went, her message was the same:

"Lots of people have different dreams, and in order to make your dreams a reality, you have to work hard. It doesn't have to be for athletics. It could be to become a doctor, a lawyer, or in everyday life. But you have to work hard. You have to be willing to make the dream a reality."

The speaking cut into her training and her personal time. Once, a group wanted Jackie to speak to them, and her calendar was full. Jackie told them that she would speak to them on her birthday. It was the only day she wasn't booked to do anything else. She believed in what she did.

"I . . . believe it is the responsibility of Olympic champions to give something back to our youth, our public. It's our duty. I realize that I've been blessed to do well in athletics. And I have had a lot of opportunities, and a lot of doors have been opened for me. I think being able to share that with someone else is a great satisfaction."

Anyone who followed Jackie around the country could see she believed in what she said about sharing and working hard. She wore a warm-up suit to the airport and worked out in the parking lot while she waited for her airplane flight.

At home, she looked for new goals in athletics. In 1989, there were no big heptathlons for Jackie to enter. So she decided to focus on jumping hurdles.

"I enjoy the sport. And I want to work toward new goals. I'm not just after Olympic titles and world records. I want to continue to excel," she said.

Jackie took off after her new goals and worked as hard as she had on the old ones. First, she tied the U.S. record in the 55-meter hurdles with a speed of 7.37 seconds. Next, she broke the U.S. record in the 60-meter hurdles at 7.81 seconds. In six U.S. straight 55-meter hurdles, no one could catch her. At the end of the season, she was the overall leader on the Mobil Grand Prix Tour.

Then came the outdoor season. Jackie entered the 400-meter hurdles to improve her performance for the heptathlon races.

"Training for one event keeps me strong in three," she said. "But I'm also taking this very seriously for its own sake."

In May 1989, she won the 400-meter hurdles at the Bruce Jenner Bud Light Classics in San Jose, California. Her speed: 57.15 seconds.

Jackie was a natural in hurdle races.

Later that year, Jackie had another big thrill: her own track meet. At the first Jackie Joyner-Kersee meet in Los Angeles, she cut her time down to 55.3 seconds.

But by the middle of the year, Jackie was worn out from traveling so much and from the events. Her asthma was bothering her more. She didn't want to take medicine for it, however, because if she did, she wouldn't be able to compete. Some of her medicine contains drugs that are not allowed in athletic competition. If she does take a dose of the medicine, it takes two to three weeks for it to leave her body. Until then, she can't enter an event.

Finally, Jackie's doctor ordered her to take time off. He said she was more than just tired. If she didn't take a real rest, she would probably get sick.

Jackie listened to the doctor and rested. She and Bob planned few events for 1990. It seemed to work. Jackie felt better. Then she realized she still wasn't well enough.

In the national outdoor championships in June, 1990, her leg muscles felt sore. She won the long jump but with a distance that was much less than her usual score—23' 2¾".

In August, Jackie won the Goodwill Games easily. But her heptathlon score was again below her standard at 6,783. Luckily, it was 547 points better than Larisa Nikitina of the Soviet Union, who came in second.

On the second day of competition, though, Jackie pulled her leg muscle and sat out the rest of the year. Then in November, 1991, Jackie had another bad asthma attack. Her lungs became infected. She developed pneumonia and had to go to the hospital.

When she came out, Jackie realized that reporters were no longer asking her when she would set a new world record or what it would be. Instead, they were asking her when she would retire and what she planned to do after she stopped competing. Jackie had already begun thinking about other careers, but she wasn't ready to retire yet.

She was only 30 years old. At 30, some athletes are too old for their sports. But many track and field athletes still compete at that age.

Jackie and Bob thought about other sports for her in case she wasn't able to do her best in the heptathlon.

Bob thought that maybe she could focus on one event.

"If she ever worked on the long jump as hard as she works on the heptathlon, she says she could long jump 25 feet, and I believe her. If she concentrated on single events, [who] knows what she's capable of doing," he said.

Jackie and Bob also talked about her trying a different sport. Babe Didrikson, one of Jackie's idols, had taken up golf after winning the gold in track and field. She became a great champion golfer.

Bob said that Arthur Ashe, the tennis champion, had once said that he would love to see what Jackie could do on a tennis court.

But both Jackie and Bob felt that she still had enough fire in her to compete in the heptathlon in the Olympics. So in June, 1991, a few weeks after an asthma attack for which she was hospitalized, Jackie started training for the national championships. Like many athletes before her, she was determined to overcome her problems.

SIDEBAR #16: OLYMPIC WOMEN

Betty Robinson: The Comeback Kid

In 1928 in Amsterdam, Elizabeth Robinson was the only American to make it to the finals in one of the new Olympic track and field events, the 100-meter race. Betty, from Riverdale, Illinois, was not one of the favorites to win.

She certainly hadn't devoted the kind of time to track and field that later women athletes would. One day she ran for the train that took her to school.

"The coach of the track team watched out of the window of the train as I caught up to it and suggested that I should develop my talent," Betty said. "Till then I didn't even know there were women's races."

Now Betty was on the field facing Fanny Rosenfeld, the front-runner, and two other women. It was a very close race, but Betty managed to edge ahead of Fanny to win the gold. A few days later, Betty helped her relay team win the silver.

Everyone thought they'd see Betty race again in the

1932 Olympics, but in 1931 she was hurt in a serious airplane accident that left her in a coma for nearly two months. When Betty finally came out of the coma, she still had to get over injuries to her arm, leg, and head.

Although, at first, Betty couldn't even bend her knee to get down on the track for the start of a race, she worked hard. In 1933, she became part of the U.S. relay team for the 1936 Olympics in Berlin.

Again, Betty and her teammates were not supposed to win. The German team had set a world record in the trial heat. But as Betty tells it, "The Germans were about ten meters ahead when I was about to pass the baton . . . then I saw the German girl throw her arms to her head and break down crying. She had dropped the baton." The U.S. team took the gold. Betty Robinson, the comeback kid, had done it again.

SIDEBAR #17: NEEDING TO WIN

Long Jumping

As part of the heptathlon and by itself, long jumping is one of Jackie's favorite events. Again, as with most of the other skills Jackie needed, speed is important in long jumping. The jumper races toward the takeoff board. She cannot stop and has to hit the board at the front. If she crosses that line without hitting it, it is a foul. But if she jumps from too far back, she will lose distance.

When Jackie first started long jumping, she

used the "hang" position. She kept her knees under her body as she jumped in the air. It is the easiest way to jump, but Bob thought she should try another way because he thought she could get more distance on her jump if she did. That way is called the "hitchkick."

In the hitchkick, the jumper runs in the air by bringing each leg forward and then back. At the end of the jump, both legs are kept straight out in front for the landing.

Some jumpers like to lift their arms in the air. Some like to use a combination of the hitchkick and the hang.

At the end of the jump, Jackie needs to reach out with her legs to get the most distance possible. The jump is measured from the nearest mark in the pit, so if she falls back or sits down in the sandpit, she can lose some distance. Even ¼" can make the difference between winning or losing, as Jackie has found out.

Chapter 11

"You Told Me to Jump . . . ."

In 1991, Jackie felt better, but she was still worried about her health. She never knew when an asthma attack might put her in the hospital. If asthma wasn't bothering her, a sore muscle or a strained hamstring could make it harder for her to compete.

Still, she and Bob went ahead with their plan: first, the national championships in New York City, then the world championships in Tokyo. The top three in the national championships would go on to make the U.S. team for the world championships. Jackie wanted to show the world that she was still a champion. As usual, she was looking ahead to the Olympics in Barcelona, Spain, in 1992.

But she downplayed her desire when she talked to reporters shortly before the national championships.

"My goal is to put myself on the team . . . without injuring myself," she said.

She started off well. In the steamy New York summer on the first day of the heptathlon competition, Jackie built up a big lead. The second day, she had pain in her groin. It and the heat caused her to finish last in the 800 meters. But she had points to spare, leading the women heptathletes with a winning score of 6,878. She made the long jump team too.

Then it was August, and Jackie and Bob arrived in Tokyo for the World Championships. Everything looked right for Jackie. She seemed back on track again.

She was happy that the long jump competition, for once, would be held before the heptathlon. She would be able to jump and then put it out of her mind. She wanted to be able to concentrate on the multievent without worrying about her jumping.

Jackie was jumping against her old friend and rival, Heike Drechsler from East Germany. By 1991, the two had become even more friendly, spending hours together on airplanes, talking about their families. But while they were friends off the field, on the field they still competed against each other. Each tried to do her best.

On her first try, Jackie hit the mark of 24'1¼"— a big jump. She was trying to get a big lead over Heike. Each jumper gets six tries. Jackie thought she could jump farther than she had.

Then, on her fourth jump, the spikes on Jackie's shoe got caught as she was about to

111

take off. Her right ankle twisted. Jackie flew through the air and landed in the pit. She was afraid she had broken her leg. Above all, she was terrified that she wouldn't be able to compete again.

Bob and Al ran to the pit. Heike ran with them. She held Jackie's head and brushed the tears and sand from her face. Finally, Jackie was sure her leg wasn't broken. It turned out to be a twisted ankle.

Jackie didn't take her fifth jump. She rested. Then Bob insisted the ankle be taped and that Jackie jump again. His thought was that Jackie had to see for herself that the ankle would be all right for the heptathlon the next day. He was also afraid that Heike might be able to improve her jump. All Heike needed to tie Jackie was to jump only an inch and a quarter farther.

Heike tried, but she couldn't do better than 23'11". Then it was Jackie's turn. The crowd couldn't believe it when she walked to the runway. She ran and then jumped for the last time in the competition.

It was not as good as her other jumps, but Jackie was able to walk away on the ankle. It had held up.

Bob was surprised that Jackie had jumped, but she said, "You told me to jump; I'm going to jump."

Jackie won the gold, and Heike congratulated her. Later, Heike said, "I should have been tougher." Yet, she wasn't sorry that she had tried to help Jackie when she fell.

The next morning, Jackie was up for the heptathlon. There was no time to rest. Before Tokyo, Jackie thought that she wanted to break 7,300 in the heptathlon. Her performance the first day looked as if she might get her wish.

She had the fastest time in the 100-meter race, she cleared over 6' 3" in the high jump, and after the shot put, had a total of 3,130 points. Everything seemed to be going her way. She was ready for the last event of the day, the 200-meter race.

Jackie had an early lead. She was coming down to the finish when she suddenly felt a terrible pain in her right leg. It was her hamstring muscle again. The weakness in her ankle had put more stress on the hamstring. Jackie tried to keep running, but she couldn't. She fell to the ground on the track and had to be taken off by stretcher.

The heptathlon was over for Jackie. Sabine Braun of Germany was the new champion heptathlete.

Again, Jackie was worried about the future, but her doctors told her that after a month of rest and recovery, she would be able to work out again.

Bob had to recover from seeing Jackie lying on the field, too. As husband and coach, he had a double load. But he says, "As soon as the husband starts to worry: 'That's my wife out there in pain,' the coach has to say: 'Shut up and get back in the stands.'"

As always, Jackie was looking ahead to the Olympics.

"I think what happened, happened for a reason," she said. "I think it will make me much hungrier, much stronger going into Barcelona, understanding that my toughest opponent is myself. I have to continue to work hard and understand that if I want to win the gold medal, I'm going to have to keep my focus."

Jackie and Bob trained hard. Jackie tried to put all her doubts behind her. But at the Olympic trials in June, 1992, Jackie let those doubts get to her. She was running the 200-meter race, the race where she had hurt her hamstring in Tokyo. When she got to the exact point where she had felt the muscle tear, she broke her stride and raised her hands, almost as if she thought she was going to fall. When she realized that her leg was all right, she started running her fastest again.

"I'm not going to defeat myself by worrying," she said. "Whatever comes, accept it." She remembered the lesson of 1984 and Glynis Nunn.

Bob knew that Jackie was worried. "She's afraid in the 200 now," he said. "Her ghost tapped her on the shoulder."

But he believed the more Jackie thought she could win, the more likely she would be to do it. The Sunday before the Olympic events, they took time off to go to a bullfight in Barcelona. A bullfight, one of Spain's national sports, puts a man, or matador, with a sword in a ring with a bull. The matador is supposed to kill the bull cleanly without making it suffer too much. Sometimes, however, the bull hurts or kills the matador. It is a very dangerous sport.

If a matador kills the bull well, he is allowed to cut off the bull's ears and tail and give them to any person he wants. In Spain, this is a great honor.

Bob and Jackie watched the bullfight for a while. Bob was interested, but Jackie hated it and cheered for the bulls. But Bob had brought Jackie there for a reason. He told her she had to think about her event like a matador and go in for the kill.

"Only thing I don't want you doing, is cutting off their ears after they're dead," he said.

As Jackie got ready for the games, she and Bob noticed how the 1992 Olympics were different. Badminton was a new Olympic sport. Politics were changing fast. The biggest news of all, however, was that the International Olympic Committee had dropped its rules that all athletes at the games be amateur. Olympic athletes could now be paid professionals—a standing that had disqualified many competitors in the past. Some had even won gold medals, like the great U.S. athlete Jim Thorpe, and then had to return them. The ruling was to change the Olympic games in many ways.

The Spanish had built 30 miles of new roads, a new airport, and had fixed up Barcelona's sports stadium. Everything was ready, and so was Jackie. The only thing that remained for her now was to see if she could bring home the gold.

Jim Thorpe: "Nobody Tackles Jim"

When Jim Thorpe was 19, he tried out for the football team at the Carlisle Indian School in 1908. The coach had Jim join the others on the team for tackling practice.

Jim was to catch the ball and try to run through the team to the goal. Most players never got very far before someone tackled them.

The team waited. Jim caught the ball. He twisted and turned as he ran, speeding past all the other boys on the field. Jim reached the goal and held up the ball. The coach couldn't believe his eyes. He had Jim do it again. Jim did the same thing.

"This was supposed to be tackling practice," the coach said to Jim.

"Nobody tackles Jim," he said to the coach.

Jim was a survivor. His twin brother had died of pneumonia. His mother died before he went to Carlisle, and his father died shortly after Jim left home. Jim had nothing and no one left but school.

He became a football hero and, in the spring, a track star. That summer, his coach suggested that he and his teammates go south and play baseball for the summer. Jim and his friends signed up to play for $25 a week. He played for several summers under his real name. Some students signed up under fake names because the Olympics did not let anyone compete who had been paid for playing sports. Jim did not know this.

In 1912, Jim was part of the U.S. Olympic team that competed in Sweden. He made news when he won the decathlon and the pentathlon with huge scores—nearly 8,413 points out of 10,000 in the decathlon and twice the point total of his nearest rival in the pentathlon.

As King Gustav of Sweden shook hands with Jim after giving him the decathlon gold medal, he said, "You, sir, are the greatest athlete in the world."

Jim didn't know what to say, so he said, "Thanks, King."

When he got back home, Jim continued his sports career in football and later baseball. But in 1913, Jim had to give back his Olympic gold medals and trophies after a newspaper reported that he had been paid for playing baseball.

The Amateur Athletic Union (AAU) asked Jim to explain.

"I didn't know that I was doing wrong," he said, "because I was doing what many other college men had done, except that they did not use their own names."

The AAU ruled that Jim had been a professional athlete at the Olympics. The International Olympic Committee demanded that Jim return his medals and erased his name from the official Olympic records.

Jim Thorpe won gold medals in the 1912 Olympics in Sweden.

Jim Thorpe puts the shot.

Jim continued playing professional sports, but as he got older, his ability faded. One newspaper story told how Jim had so little money he couldn't afford to buy a ticket for the 1932 Olympics in Los Angeles.

During his life and after he died in 1952, Jim's family and friends tried to get the Olympic Committee to restore Jim's medals and records. In 1982, the Committee voted yes. In January of the following year, new medals were presented to his children.

SIDEBAR #19: OLYMPIC WOMEN

Wyomia Tyus: Two-Time Champion

One of the few women to equal Jackie's record of Olympic medals was Wyomia Tyus, the first winner of two straight Olympic sprint titles.

Born in Griffin, Georgia to a father who was a dairy worker and a mother who worked in a laundry, Wyomia loved playing basketball. When basketball season ended, Wyomia was at loose ends. So she joined the track and field team and became their top sprinter.

Then, at age 15, two important things happened to Wyomia. First, her father died. Wyomia was the only girl in the family, and she had been especially close to her father. He became her inspiration.

Also, she was invited to be part of a track and field summer program at Tennessee State University. Not only was her talent recognized there, but the coaches kept an eye on her for the future. Wyomia received an athletic scholarship from Tennessee State after she graduated from high school.

From Tennessee State, Wyomia began setting new records every year. In 1964, at the Tokyo Olympics, she set a new Olympic and world record in the 100-meter dash. That was her first Olympic gold. She also won a silver medal in the 4×100 relay.

For the next four years, Wyomia continued to smash records. Then in 1968, in Mexico City, she did it all over again, winning the 100-meters and the 4 × 100 relay for two gold medals.

Later, Wyomia became a teacher, coach, and a TV commentator. She's worked with the U.S. Olympic Committee and was a Goodwill Ambassador to Africa. The 100-meter sprint had taken her far.

Chapter 12

A New World

Each Olympics is different. But this time, the map of the world had changed from 1988 to 1992. While some of the same athletes had entered the games, they were competing for different teams. Europe, with the fall of Communism, was becoming a new world. The Olympic teams showed it.

The Berlin Wall, which had separated West Germany from East Germany, had been torn down. Easterners and Westerners, who had not been able to live together or talk with each other for many years, were now on the same Olympic team.

Yugoslavia, Bosnia-Herzegovina, Slovenia, and Croatia, once united, were all fighting each other. Each sent its own team.

The Soviet Union had collapsed. Its twelve republics were allowed to form a one-time-only Unified Team. After that, they were expected to form their own teams.

Europe was not the only part of the globe where changes were taking place. South Africa, having dismantled its apartheid system, was welcomed back to the Olympics. The last time it had competed was 1960.

When the winners of the women's 10,000-meter race were announced, it was noted that two Africans had taken first and second place. Deratu Tulu of Ethiopia became the first black African woman to win a gold medal in an Olympic competition. The silver medal went to Elana Meyer, a white runner from South Africa. Both women ran their victory lap, the run winners take around the track, together.

"We both ran for Africa," said Elana, after the race. "I think we did that very well."

Some athletes had political problems. Some had other kinds of problems. Jackie's teammate, Gail Devers, had overcome terrible illness to get to Barcelona. Gail, a sprinter, had been suffering from Graves' disease and, at one time, was told she might have to have her feet cut off.

Mark Spitz, the U.S. swimmer who had won seven gold medals in 1972, was determined at the age of 42 to compete in the Olympics again. This time he had his sights set on winning just one gold medal in the 100-meter butterfly. Most people thought he was too old to compete.

"I am probably in the best shape . . . physically than anybody my age," he said. "I don't care what sport you're talking about."

123

Carl Lewis had no worries. The track and field champion had already won six gold medals—four at Los Angeles in 1984, two at Seoul in 1988. He knew he could jump and sprint with the best. Now he was competing against Mike Powell—another U.S. champion—who had broken the world's long jump record with a leap of 29' 4½" in Tokyo in 1991. That didn't bother Carl. After Mike had broken the record, reporters asked Carl how he felt.

"Somebody was just telling me that it's not time to stop jumping yet," he said.

For Heike Drechsler, it was another chance to compete against Jackie in the long jump and to see if she could win a medal in the high jump.

Worried, excited, all the athletes gathered in Barcelona's stadium with a crowd of 100,000, while two billion more people watched the opening of the Olympic Games on television. An archer shot a flaming arrow and lit the Olympic torch to open the games. After that, humans and an ocean full of make-believe monsters acted out a battle with each other. Famous opera singers performed too.

Finally, the games began. Jackie got off to a fast start the first day by winning the 100-meter hurdles. But her nearest competition, Sabine Braun of Germany, beat her by one inch in the high jump. By this time, Jackie was upset, and the shot put didn't help. Her best throw landed four inches behind Sabine's.

An archer shoots a flaming arrow to light the Olympic rings in Barcelona, 1992.

But Jackie pulled herself together and won the 200-meter with a time of 23.12 seconds. Sabine managed to get 24.27. Now she was 127 points behind Jackie.

Sabine's teammates were determined that she win. When most athletes get ready before an event, they try to concentrate. They think about what they will do and how they will do it. The German women's team tried to break Jackie's concentration. They were very upset that she was doing so well.

Jackie laughed about it, but Bob was angry. "Every time they try to intimidate Jackie, it's going to cost them an Olympic medal."

Bob knew that now was not the time to yell at Jackie. He wanted her to relax.

"I told her to go out and have fun, to enjoy herself," he said.

The next day, Jackie's long jump of 23' 3½" gave her the lead and got her 1,206 points. After the javelin throw and the 800-meter, Jackie had done it again. She had scored 7,044. Irina Belova of the Unified Team was second with a score of 6,845. And Sabine Braun? She ended up with the bronze.

Jackie's win was not an easy one. After the 800-meter run, she had an asthma attack. Her fans were worried when she did not come out for a victory lap after her win.

They chanted "Jackie! Jackie!" until she got her breath back and was able to come out.

"I felt like the baseball player who comes back out of the dugout after hitting a home run," she said. "I was tired, but . . . I had to take that victory lap and shake hands with those people."

She also thought that the crowd would never chant for her. "Hardly anyone ever watches the heptathlon. I never thought that it would happen to me."

Jackie had time to rest before the long jump competition began. There, she faced her old friend, Heike Drechsler, again. This time the outcome was different from 1988. Then Heike had lost to Jackie, who won the gold medal. This time, Heike won. Jackie's jump of 23' 2½" was enough to give her the bronze.

But Jackie's place in the history books was assured. She became the first female athlete in a multievent to win back-to-back gold medals at the Olympic Games.

For Jackie it only equalled the thrill that she got when her hero, Bruce Jenner, took her aside to pay her a compliment. Bruce was the man she had watched on TV when he won the gold in the 1976 decathlon. At the time she had been a poor girl thousands of miles and a world away in East St. Louis. Now he said to her, "You have proved to the world that you are the greatest athlete who ever lived, male or female. You have done what no one has ever done."

Later, he described her to others at Barcelona as simply "the best who's ever lived."

Jackie won the gold in the heptathlon in Barcelona.

It was a wonderful Olympics for Jackie. But what of the other athletes who had come there with such high hopes?

Just a year before, in 1991, Gail Devers' legs started to swell from the treatments she was receiving for Graves' disease, a thyroid problem. The doctors thought they might have to cut off her feet. But the doctors decided to wait, and the swelling went down.

In the 100-meter final, Gail was not the favorite to win. Most people thought another American woman, Gwen Torrence, would win it. But Gail's motto was, "You should never give up." Gail breezed by Gwen and the other runners to finish in first place. Gwen Torrence was so surprised she couldn't believe it. She accused Gail of taking drugs to speed up her running. But Gail was clean. Bob Kersee, who was Gail's coach as well as Jackie's, ran out onto the track after the race and hugged her.

Then Gail got ready for the 100-meter hurdles. She was on her way to winning when she tripped on the last hurdle, fell to the ground, and ended up in fifth place. The winner of the hurdles, Paraskevi Patoulidou, made history as the first Greek woman ever to win the gold.

Mark Spitz, the great Olympic swimmer, found his conditioning wasn't good enough. He lost the race in the butterfly by 1.78 seconds—too much time to be even close to coming in third. His day as an Olympic swimmer was over.

Carl Lewis started off the Olympics in poor health. He had a virus and dropped out of the sprint competition. Other U.S. athletes were favorites to win the sprint because Carl was not running. But in a surprise upset, British runner Linford Christie won. Linford had such poor training habits that he was called an "athletic layabout."

Carl recovered and focused on his other events. He was determined to show Mike Powell that he was still king of the long jump. He took off and landed a jump of 28' 5½" to win over Powell's 28' 4½". Powell held the world record, but he knew that Carl Lewis could still jump with the best.

"The rest of the world may see Carl Lewis a couple times a year," he said, "but we think about him every day."

As for Jackie, she was thinking about other careers and looking ahead to the 1996 Olympics. Did she think that at 34 she might be too old to compete in the next Olympic Games to be held in Atlanta?

"No, I believe age is only a state of mind," she said.

But she knew that more hard work lay ahead of her.

"Women in sports now receive equal recognition," she said. "But they still have to work twice as hard as men to be recognized."

SIDEBAR #20: HIGHLIGHTS OF THE 1992 SUMMER OLYMPICS: BARCELONA

• At the first modern Olympics in 1896 in Athens, there were 200 participants—all men—from 14 countries. There were 43 events. In 1992, at the summer Olympics, 9,364 athletes competed—6,657 men, 2,707 women—from 169 countries. Events totaled 257.

• Lithuania—one of the former Soviet republics—had not competed in the Olympics since 1928 and had never won a medal. Discus thrower Romas Ubartas brought home the gold for the first time.

• The United States, renowned for baseball, came in a surprising fourth after Cuba, Chinese Taipei, and Japan.

• For the first time, badminton became an Olympic sport. Two Indonesians, Allan Budi Kusma in the men's and Susi Susanti, his fiancée, in the women's, won the gold. The badminton competition was very popular, and millions watched it on TV around the world.

• Twice, Heike Henkel of Germany missed the high jump of 6' 5½".

• Everyone thought she had no chance of winning. But on her very last try, Heike jumped 6' 7¼" to win the gold.

• In volleyball, the American men's team shaved their heads to protest poor calls by the referee in a game. They brought home a bronze medal.

SIDEBAR #21: OLYMPIC WOMEN

Yael Arad: In Their Honor

Although Baron de Coubertin wanted the Olympics to be dedicated to peace, there have been times when the Games have been remembered for terror.

In 1972, at the Olympic Games in Munich, Germany, eight men from the Black September terrorist group carried out a mission to hold the Israeli men's team as hostages. In return, the group wanted Israel to release two hundred Arab prisoners from jail.

Killing two Israelis, the terrorists took nine of the team hostage. The terrorists demanded a jet to take them and their captives away. When some of the terrorists came out of hiding to look for the jet, sharpshooters tried to hit them. The terrorists fought back. When the battle ended, five terrorists were dead along with the entire Israeli wrestling and weight-lifting team.

In 1992, at Barcelona, Yael Arad became the first Israeli athlete to win an Olympic medal. She dedicated it to the eleven Israeli athletes who had been murdered at Munich.

She began taking judo lessons with her brother when she was eight. At ten, she won the Israeli championship for her age group. Even though she had a knee operation four months before Barcelona, Yael was determined to compete. She came very close to winning the gold but was edged out by Catherine Fleury of France.

Yael Arad won a silver medal for Israel in 1992.

Yael hopes to encourage more Jewish children to get involved with sports. Like Jackie, she has started a foundation for young athletes.

"Sport is the purest thing," she says. "When you win in sports, it has nothing to do with politics."

Chapter 13

Battling Her Body

After Barcelona, Bruce Jenner wasn't the only one to recognize Jackie's achievements. Columnist Jim Murray in *The Los Angeles Times* wrote: " . . . the world's greatest athlete may very well be just a slip of a girl and not a hunk at all—just 5' 10" and 155—who can cook, has brown eyes and a nice smile, and a figure that could make a chorus line."

Washington University, in her hometown of St. Louis, Missouri, gave her an honorary Doctor of Law degree. The Women's Sports Foundation named her its Amateur Sportswoman of the Year for the third time. *Women's Sports & Fitness* also said: "[She's] also the sportswoman of the decade, the century, and the millennium." In *Newsweek,* Frank Deford wrote of her: "If Joyner-Kersee had been a male, she'd have been a lottery pick in the NBA [National Basketball Association], made many millions a year, and probably never gone near a track." The praise and the honors would have made a wonderful ending to anyone's career. But Jackie wasn't done yet.

In August, 1993, Jackie won a second World Championship in the heptathlon. This time, Jackie wasn't only competing against Sabine Braun, she was battling against her own body. Sick with a fever, Jackie knew she had to catch up with Sabine, who was leading by seven points. In the final 800-meter run, Jackie forced herself to run faster than Sabine, speeding up at the end of the race to give her competitor what Bob called "a knockout blow." Jackie won the gold again with 6,837 points to Sabine's 6,797.

On March 5, 1994, at the National Indoor Track and Field Championships, she smashed her 1992 American long jump record with a new jump of 23' 4¾". Jackie was thrilled, but later in the meet, while running and jumping the 60-meter hurdles, she hit a hurdle hard with her left foot. Jackie thought she had broken her foot, but, luckily, it was just badly bruised.

There were other signs that her body—so long able to do just what she told it to—was breaking down. In May, 1994, she won the long jump at the New York Games. But she did it on her first jump because she had decided not to take a second one.

"I was so excited, I was wheezing," she said. "I thought, I don't want to have an asthma attack out here." Other times, as she was racing, the asthma was so bad that she saw little white lights before her eyes.

She started training differently. "Mostly I try to preserve her body now," said Bob. "I have her riding a bike, swimming in a pool. I have her running in the pool. You see, I fool her body to make her stronger with less stress on the joints.

Jackie didn't always agree with what Bob was doing, but "I can't push myself enough, so I need Bob for that. If I'm going to win the Olympics this year [1996], I know I have to do everything right. I can't let my pride and my ego get in the way."

Their partnership as husband and wife and coach and athlete continued to be a happy one.

"As a coach, it's my privilege working with her—like working with . . . Michael Jordan. I remind her that I'm like the Secret Service with the president. She may be the boss, but it's my job to make decisions about what's best for her. And if she doesn't like it—all right, fire me, Jackie."

But both Bob and Jackie were looking ahead. Jackie would be competing in the Olympics at age 34. Both of them were thinking about starting a family.

"I am not going to raise any child of mine on a track," said Jackie.

"One day, I want to stand at a finish line with our children and tell them: 'Watch, because I saw your mother win this once,'" says Bob.

First, however, came the 1994 Goodwill Games—always a success story for Jackie. This time, though, trouble came first. On July 26, in the sixth round of the heptathlon, Jackie was almost thrown out of the competition for a sticky javelin. A Russian judge said that Jackie had put something on her javelin so she could hold it more firmly for a better throw.

Jackie told him that the javelin was sticky from beer, which a fan had spilled on it. She had told her competitors about it, and the Russian judges had approved her javelin.

Jane Frederick said it was just another try by her competitors to upset Jackie before the event. And just before the javelin throw the judges told her that what they had said to her was just a warning. Jackie was still in the competition.

Bob was angry. He thought the Russians should have said they were sorry to Jackie. "You just don't do that to a world champion and three-time Goodwill Games winner."

Jackie finished fifth in the javelin and last in the 800-meter race. During the race, she had another asthma attack.

Her Goodwill Games string of successes held. Jackie had won the heptathlon again—this time with a score of 6,606 points. She continued on, winning the long jump event in the IVO Van Damme Memorial in Brussels, Belgium, and the Grand Prix Final in Paris, France. Again, she was in pain—with a strained right hamstring.

Still Jackie was happy. "I think this fills a gap in my career. This is a really great end to my season," she said.

Along with her athletic career, Jackie started helping Bob with other athletes. Tennis star Monica Seles had been knifed in the back by a disturbed man. The man was a fan of another tennis star, Steffi Graf, and thought if he hurt Monica, Steffi would win. After being knifed, Monica took time off to pull herself together and decide if she wanted to play tennis again. When she made up her mind that she did want to continue her tennis career, Jackie helped Bob train Monica.

However, Jackie wasn't ready to give up her own athletic ambitions yet. Despite all her pain and strains, she was looking forward to Atlanta.

"Nothing would be greater than to finish my career on American soil," she said. "As you get older, you see younger people ready to take your place. But that's also my motivation. It keeps my fire going to see girls coming after me."

First, she had to qualify for the Olympics. In the past, it had been no problem for Jackie to come out of the Olympic trials as part of the U.S. team—one of the three athletes with top scores in the heptathlon.

This time, Jackie struggled. Sportswriters pointed out that Jackie, at age 34, was getting older, her competition was younger, she hadn't competed in a heptathlon in a year, and she hadn't scored over 7,000 points since 1992 in the Olympics.

Jackie was determined to show them she could still compete and win. Her main competition was Kelly Blair, from Prosser, Washington. Kelly, who had graduated from high school with honors, had also won the NCAA championship in Oregon.

When it came to the long jump, Jackie did well, as always. Kelly fouled on her first two jumps. She had one jump left. If she missed, she would be out of the competition. Jackie waited to see what would happen. Kelly jumped and made it.

It was coming down to the last part of the heptathlon—the final 800-meter race. Jackie was ahead by 116 points. If she could just hold on, she could not only win but be the leader of the team of three for the Olympics.

Jackie ran as hard as she could, but her asthma started bothering her. Kelly beat her by 8.57 seconds. When the final scores were added up, Kelly was the top finisher with 6,406. She had beaten Jackie by three points. Both women would be going on to the Olympics. But the final scores made both Jackie and Bob think. It was Jackie's second lowest heptathlon score since 1983. Her asthma seemed to be bothering her more and more.

Yet Bob felt that Jackie could still win at the Olympics. When reporters asked him about Jackie's performance, he said: "There's nothing physically wrong with Jackie. She had technical problems and left points all over that stadium."

Jackie, herself, felt she had to work harder. "I can't come to the Olympic Games and perform at this level. I just can't."

So Jackie continued to practice from early morning to early evening—running, jumping, throwing, and lifting. Bob was beside her, as always, telling her what to do every minute.

Both of them were looking ahead to what might be. What if Jackie won the gold again?

"Three times in a row?" said Bob. "Winning three times in a row with four years in between in a competition that requires the mastery of several disciplines. That's amazing. It's absolutely amazing."

Only Jackie, Bob Mathias, and Daley Thompson had won gold medals for multievents two Olympics in a row. Three times would be astounding. But as the time came nearer for the Olympics in Atlanta, that's what Jackie decided she would try to do.

SIDEBAR #22: ATLANTA AND THE OLYMPICS

As soon as it was known that Atlanta, Georgia had won the vote to host the first games of the second century of the Olympics, the city got busy. It had to raise over $1.5 billion to build athletic sites worthy of the games. Big companies chipped in, and much of the money was raised from TV coverage. There was a lot to see even before the Olympics began.

The torch was carried from Greece to the U.S. There it was passed from city to city—sometimes carried by athletes, sometimes by people who had made a difference in some way, sometimes by the famous, and sometimes by those who were known only in their hometowns. Jackie, herself, carried the torch to a ceremony beneath St. Louis's

Gateway Arch—a long, shining arc that is the pride of the city. Finally, the torch arrived in Atlanta.

Over 10,000 athletes showed up with it, along with at least two million visitors. They were greeted by steaming heat—over 90 degrees on many days—and musical celebrities—like Ray Charles, Gloria Estefan, B. B. King, and Stevie Wonder—as well as outstanding athletic performances.

Some visitors tested themselves against special exhibits where they could pretend to race against Jackie Joyner-Kersee or match their skills against other Olympic athletes. Others spent their time trading Olympic pins that featured different teams and countries. Still others tried different foods like cornbread and greens, as new to them as their native foods would be to us.

Then there were the main attractions. Some were old favorites—long jumper Carl Lewis, who at 35 wanted to prove he could still win a gold medal; and newcomers like Michael Johnson, fighting for the title of fastest man in the world. There were new events—women's teams for basketball and softball.

There was joy and there was sorrow—not only for those athletes who did not win. On the ninth day of the seventeen devoted to the games, July 27th, a pipe bomb hidden in a green knapsack went off in the early hours of the morning. The bomb shook an area of three city blocks. One woman was killed by the blast. A cameraman, running to film the horrible event, died of a heart attack. More than 100 people were hurt.

For many, it was a reminder of the eleven Israelis who had been killed at the Munich Olympics. For others, it was a reminder that no place—not even the Olympics—was safe from terrorists.

As Canadian rower Silken Laumann said, "It's sad that something that is supposed to be about peace and fair play becomes a target like this."

At the end, Atlanta Mayor Bill Campbell said of the games, " . . . they were the largest, with the most athletes, the most female athletes, the most nations, and we think the Games were very successful. We will allow historians to judge."

SIDEBAR #23: OLYMPIC MEN

Josia Thugwane: Out of South Africa

At 17, Josia Thugwane was a good soccer player, but he was small. He knew a small man wouldn't do well in professional soccer, so he tried to find another sport. As a black man living in a poor township in South Africa, Josia knew that hard work would be the only way he might be able to lift himself out of poverty. He found out that road races paid money, but he had no running shoes.

"I didn't have the money for new shoes, but there was a guy, he had a pair of shoes, the same size as mine. He said he would sell them to me for . . . about $40. They had not been used much. He said he would let me pay a little bit, then a little bit, then a little bit. I ran races, and if I won any money, I gave it to him for the shoes. The final payment, I won . . . by winning half a marathon."

Later, Josia worked out the same agreement with shoe shops. His running got him a job in a gold mine. He had no coach. He had an agent who tried to get him races, but mostly Josia was on his own.

He started winning. He made the South African Olympic marathon team.

Everything looked bright for Josia. Then five months before the Olympics, he was shot after being carjacked near his hometown. Luckily, the bullet just grazed his chin. But his new fame had made him and his family targets for robbers and thugs.

When Josia and his teammates left for the U.S., they were afraid that criminals might try to hurt their families or hold them for ransom. It was hard for them to think only of training and running.

When the day of the marathon came, the men on the team were not sure who would have the best chance of winning. But after 2 hours, 12 minutes and 36 seconds, a 25 year-old, 5' 2" man weighing 97 pounds ran to the finish line. It was Josia. He had become the first black South African to win an Olympic gold medal.

South African President Nelson Mandela called him "our golden boy" and "a worthy role model." Josia took his victory lap wearing sunglasses and holding high the new flag of his country.

"This is for my country," he said. "This is for my president. I'm grateful that I have this opportunity. It is an indication to others that if we work hard, all of us have equal opportunity, not like in the past."

SIDEBAR #24: OLYMPIC MEN

Muhammad Ali: "About The Human Spirit"

Dressed in white, he stepped out of the darkness to light the torch and open the 26th Summer Olympics in Atlanta. More than three billion people saw his hands shake as he slowly leaned over to light the Olympic flame. That was when the world learned that the great boxing champion had Parkinson's disease, a disease of the nerves.

"Like everyone else in that stadium, I was deeply moved," said NBC-TV commentator Bob Costas. "Here's a guy who was once the most alive of men— the most dynamic and beautiful athlete we'd ever known—and now, to an extent, he was imprisoned by Parkinson's. His lighting that torch said something about the human spirit."

An Olympic gold medalist and the only man to win the world heavyweight boxing championship three times, Muhammad Ali might never have become a boxer if his new red bicycle hadn't been stolen when he was 14. He reported the theft to policeman Joe Martin, who also gave kids boxing lessons. Martin never got Muhammad's bike back, but he did recruit him for boxing.

"He was just ordinary," said Martin, "but he was easily the hardest worker of any kid I ever taught.

Muhammad rose at 5 A.M. to run in the park. Instead of taking the bus to school, he ran alongside it for 28 blocks. At lunch, he ran again. In the evening, he worked out at Martin's gym.

But after winning the national Golden Gloves and the AAU light-heavyweight championships, as well as the 1960 Olympics, he was still refused service at downtown restaurants in his hometown of Louisville, Kentucky because of his color.

"I don't care what he's won," said one luncheonette owner. "He can't eat here."

But nothing stopped Muhammad Ali. When some people resented his decision to become a Muslim, he was steadfast in his faith; he still prays five times a day.

When he refused to be inducted into the Army, saying his religion forbade him to bear arms, many people called him a draft dodger. The government charged him with draft evasion and he faced a prison sentence. Boxing officials stripped him of his title. For three and a half years, he didn't box. Yet, even after he was convicted of draft evasion and sentenced to five years in jail and a $10,000 fine, he remained firm.

Eventually, his case went to the Supreme Court, and he won. He had to sue to regain his right to box. When he won that battle, he immediately tried to get his title back, fighting the heavyweight champion, Joe Frazier. Although Muhammad

Muhammad Ali

fought bravely, he lost.

Finally, in 1974 in Zaire, Muhammad knocked out George Foreman in the eighth round.

Today, although he suffers from Parkinson's, he's on the road 275 days a year for charity benefits.

"Everything I do, I say to myself, 'Will God accept this?'. . . . I love going to hospitals. I love sick people. I don't worry about disease. Allah will protect me. He always does."

Chapter 14

Atlanta and Beyond

Muhammed Ali had lit the torch. The opening ceremonies were over. Now it was time for 10,000 athletes to get to work.

Each had a story. Each one had dreams and desires. There was Carl Lewis. At age 35, he had barely made the U.S. team. Yet, he had won four gold medals in 1984, two in 1988, and two in 1992. This time, most people thought he would be lucky if he won a bronze medal for the long jump.

Carl, however, had other ideas: " . . . every time somebody has told me I couldn't do something, I've done it."

He showed them. When the long jump event was over, Carl had jumped an amazing 27' 10¾" to beat twelve other athletes and win his ninth gold medal.

"That's it," he said. "There's no way I can top this. I look forward to life after track and field because there are other things outside of track that are passionate to me—my charity work, speaking to young people, getting more involved in political issues. These are the kind of things I'm looking forward to doing."

There was Dot Richardson. At age 34, this was her first Olympics. Dot was part of the U.S. women's softball team, which was allowed to play for the first time in the games. It was something Dot had dreamed about for 20 years.

As a little girl, she had wanted to play baseball, but the Little League coach had told her that she couldn't play unless she cut her hair and called herself Bob. At age 15, Dot had been asked to play in a women's professional softball league but chose to remain an amateur in case she could play in the Olympics some day.

Later, Dot went to UCLA—Jackie's college—on a softball scholarship. When she graduated, she went to medical school in Kentucky. Now she had taken a year off from being a doctor to get ready for the Olympics. As soon as the games were over, she was due back in the hospital operating room.

To prepare for the Olympics, Dot practiced batting late at night after she had come home to her apartment from working in the hospital. One morning she found a note taped to her door. It was from her neighbors. The note said:

"If you're going to train for the Olympics, please do it at a decent hour."

The neighbors were joking. They didn't realize that Dot *was* training for the Olympics.

And they were probably among the thousands who cheered when Dot and the U.S. team came away with the first-ever gold medal in women's softball. It was a victory with a lot of meaning for Dot, especially when she thought about the girls who might follow in her footsteps.

"I see a look in their eyes that they will never be the same again," she said, "that they now know they can be an Olympian. And that through softball they can receive an education and actually achieve a lot of their dreams."

For Michael Johnson, 1996 was the year of the payback. In the 1992 Olympics, he had been ready to sprint but had gotten sick with food poisoning. His coach, Clyde Hart, said, "You have to understand, Michael's been on a four-year mad ever since Barcelona." He was determined to win both the 200- and the 400-meter sprints.

Slipping on gold shoes especially made for him for the Olympics, Michael took an early lead in the 200-meter race.

"I saw a blue blur go by, whoosh," said Ato Boldon of Trinidad, "and thought, 'There goes first.'" Boldon ended up with the bronze.

Then Michael passed Frankie Fredericks of Namibia, who would finish second. It was only 19.32 seconds after the start that Michael broke the tape of the finish line. He had also broken his own world record and had become the first man ever to win both the 200- and 400-meter Olympic races.

Later, reporters asked him how it felt to go faster than any man had ever gone before.

"It was like the first time I went down the hill at the end of our street in the go-cart my father made for me," he said. "If you want to know what that's like, get yourself a go-cart."

For Michael Johnson, Jackie Joyner-Kersee, Gail Devers, and other track and field stars, the fans who turned out to see them in Atlanta were a surprise. No longer did Jackie have to tell people she competed in the heptathlon and explain what she did. Morning sessions at the Olympics, sessions that weren't even finals, drew more than 80,000 interested people, who wanted to watch their favorites.

"I was always told Americans weren't interested in track and field," said Roger Black, a British sprinter. "Then I go out and see 80,000 people in the morning."

Jackie wanted to show them what she could do. After her disappointing second-place finish in the trials, she said, "I'm not going out this way. I've worked too hard this year, and I'd like to see it pay off."

She was ready. But in the first event of the heptathlon, the 100-meter hurdles, Bob knew something was wrong before the fourth hurdle. Jackie had a look of terrible pain on her face. She finished the race, but she had pulled her right hamstring again.

No one could help her. At other meets, sports trainers and others are there to help the athlete who hurts herself. They can give her first-aid and help her pull through the race mentally as well. But at the Olympics, such help is off-limits because of security reasons.

Jackie wanted to continue on, but Bob knew that she could hurt herself for good by doing so. If Jackie were to race with this kind of injury, she might never be able to compete again.

"I'm going to have to pull you out," he said to her. "This is your husband talking, not your coach." Then they hugged each other and cried together. Jackie and Bob's dreams of winning a third gold medal in the heptathlon had died.

Jackie decided she would try to rest and get better. Maybe, just maybe, she would be able to compete in her other event—the long jump.

In the meantime, Bob was busy with other Olympic athletes. Gail Devers, the woman who thought she might never run again because of her illness, was now competing in the 100-meter sprint. Her competition was tough. There was Marlene Ottey of Jamaica. Marlene had won four bronze medals in four different Olympics. And there was Gwen Torrence—the 1995 world champion and the woman that Gail had beaten in Barcelona just four years before.

Gwen had not been happy about losing to Gail and had accused her of taking drugs. Gail was clean. This time, Gwen was racing in her hometown—Atlanta. She wanted to thrill the hometown crowd and win the gold.

The three runners took off with Gail leading. After her, came Marlene, and then Gwen. As they neared the finish line, Gail twisted her shoulder forward and put her head down. Marlene kept her chest forward.

It was Barcelona all over again. Marlene and Gail had finished so close together that no one knew who won. The women and their fans waited. Finally, the finish was shown on the big screen in the stadium. Gail had won, although she and Marlene both had the same time— 10.94. Gwen had come in third.

Bob was there to celebrate with Gail. He ran from the sidelines, grabbed her and swung her around.

This time, Marlene was not happy. The Jamaican Federation protested for Marlene, saying that Gail should not win just because her head crossed the finish line first. But the judges said that Gail was the winner. She had won the gold medal for the 100-meter sprint in back-to-back Olympics.

In a surprise move, Gail and Gwen took a victory lap together around the track. In the spirit of the Olympics, all had been forgiven.

"We're competitors, not rivals," Gail said to reporters.

"When it's over, it's over," said Gwen. "I am ecstatic to get a medal."

Then Gail, remembering the bomb that had hurt so many people, said, "It's a time for me to be joyous about what I did. But it's also a time for sadness."

Meanwhile, Jackie rested and took advantage of physical therapy. She wanted to leave her mark on this Olympics, but she wasn't sure she would be able to pull herself together.

Five days after her disappointment in the heptathlon, she taped herself up and went out for the long jump. Five jumps later, she was still trying. She got ready for her sixth and last jump. She was in sixth place before the jump. This was her last chance to win a medal.

She said to herself, "This is it, Jackie, this is it. This isn't the way you wanted it to be, but this is your last shot."

Jackie knew she would have to take her chances that she might pull her hamstring again. She took off and prayed that if she pulled the hamstring, she would pull it in the air where it wouldn't hurt her jump.

She landed the jump at 22' 11¾"—and won the bronze medal by one inch.

Jackie, the most decorated Olympic woman of all time, said, "Of all the medals I've won, I really had to work for this one. This one really tested me as far as my determination and my will to really want it. I really don't like pain, and I was in a lot of pain."

It was a fitting end for a woman who had been called "the greatest athlete of all time."

Now it was time for Jackie to start a new life. Like many other professional athletes, she had started to make plans for another career. She

Jackie won the bronze in the long jump at the 1996 Olympics.

knew that she would not be able to compete in the heptathlon forever.

Most of her choices still centered on sports.

"I've tried golf, and I've learned that it's a lot harder than it looks. But it is something I want to do a lot of . . . ," she said. She also talked about competing in hurdling and the long jump.

Finally, in the fall of 1996, Jackie announced that she would play in the American Basketball

League (ABL), the new women's league, as a forward for the Richmond Rage. Jackie was going back to one of her first loves—basketball. She would also be an ambassador for the new league and would still compete in track.

Jackie could also take the time to relax and enjoy herself. She had been awarded a lifetime pass for free meals at McDonald's. Her favorite food was a double cheeseburger with extra mustard, and she would be on the road enough—traveling—to enjoy many.

As always, Jackie would devote herself to her foundation and to reaching out to children.

"I like kids to get to know me. Sure, I've achieved a lot, but the thing is to let them see that everyone is raw material. I want to be a good statement of the possibilities."

And she would continue to be a competitor as well as a role model for younger athletes. In June 1997, Jackie again competed at the U.S. track and field championships in Indianapolis. This time, she leaped 22' 8" in her fifth try in the long jump. But Marion Jones, fourteen years younger, beat her by one inch to take first place. As always, Jackie's competitors become her friends. She and Marion hugged on the runway after the event was over.

" . . . it was very motivating competing against Jackie. I knew she'd come back and jump a big one," Marion said.

"Even though she's 21 and I'm 35, I have the fight in me to compete," Jackie said. "Someone as gifted as she is, hopefully, will make us better. I'm very glad to see someone like Marion. To have young athletes coming up who are not immature in their actions on and off the field lends a lot of credibility to track and field."

Who knows what the future holds for Jackie? All things are possible. For against the odds— death of loved ones, poverty, illness—time after time, Jackie has succeeded. Her dreams have been more than fulfilled.

"I just wanted to be an Olympian," she said. "In my dreams I never envisioned people asking for my autograph, going to the White House, being able to travel the world, meeting different people. Or being able to have a house or car. . . . I never thought I would be like that. It's been a blessing because I keep in mind how I got it. Not to take anything for granted."

SIDEBAR #25: TIMELINE

Life and Triumphs of Jackie Joyner-Kersee

1962–Born March 3 in East St. Louis, Illinois to Mary and Alfred Joyner

1971–Starts basketball, volleyball, and track and field at Mary E. Brown Community Center; meets Coach Nino Fennoy

1976–Wins National Championship in the pentathlon at the Junior Olympics

From left to right: Jackie's Aunt Della; her sister, Angela; Jackie; and her brother, Al

1977–Wins Junior Olympics pentathlon National Championship for the second time; Featured in *Sports Illustrated;* enters high school and joins basketball, volleyball, and track and field teams

1978–Wins pentathlon National Championship for the third time

1979–Becomes captain of the high school basketball, volleyball, and track teams; basketball and track teams win state championship; named All-State and All-American in track and basketball; invited to try out for the 1980 Olympic Long Jump Team

1980–Enters UCLA with a basketball scholarship; finds out she has asthma

1981–Jackie's mother, Mary Joyner, dies; Bob Kersee begins coaching Jackie in the heptathlon; Jackie wins the Broderick Award as the U.S. top athlete in college

1982–Wins two top heptathlete awards; sets new NCAA record; honored as UCLA All-University Athlete in basketball and track

1983–Named most valuable player on the UCLA basketball team; wins NCAA heptathlon championship a second time; Most Valuable Player on the women's track team; All-University athlete again; makes U.S. track and field team for World Championships along with her brother, Al

1984–Sets new U.S. indoor record in the long jump; wins heptathlon at the Olympic Trials and sets new U.S. record; wins silver medal in the heptathlon at the Olympics

1985–Named UCLA's All-University Athlete for a third time; wins the Broderick Cup; at the National Sports Festival, wins all seven heptathlon events for the first time

1986–Marries Bob Kersee on January 11; at the Goodwill Games, is the first woman to break the world record in the heptathlon, then does it again at the Olympic Sports Festival; wins the Jesse Owens Memorial Award, the Sullivan Award, and *Track and Field News'* Athlete of the Year

1987–Wins the heptathlon and ties the world long jump record at the Pan-American Games; wins gold medals in the heptathlon and the long jump at the World Championships; wins awards from the Women's Sports Foundation and the Associated Press; receives the Jesse Owens Memorial Award for the second time; wins the National Outdoor Championships heptathlon and long jump titles

1988–Scores more than 7,000 points in the heptathlon for the fourth time at the Olympic Trials; Wins a gold medal in the heptathlon and another in the long jump at the Olympics; Sets a new Olympic record in the long jump and a new world record in the 800-meter; establishes the Jackie Joyner-Kersee Community Foundation in East St. Louis

1991–Wins the gold medal in the long jump at the World Championships

1992–Wins the heptathlon in the Olympic Trials; wins gold medals at the Goodwill Games in the heptathlon and the long jump; receives honorary Doctor of Law degree from Washington University in St. Louis; wins the heptathlon gold at the Olympics

1993–Wins the World Outdoor Championship heptathlon; becomes McDonald's Amateur Athlete of the Year

1994–Wins the 100-meter hurdles at the Olympic Festival; breaks her own U.S. record in the long jump at the National Indoor Track and Field

Championships; wins the high jump and the 60-meter hurdles at the Millrose Games; wins her third straight gold medal in the heptathlon at the Goodwill Games; wins the long jump event at the Van Damme Memorial and at the Grand Prix Final

1996–Wins the bronze medal in the long jump at the Olympics; joins the Richmond Rage as a forward and becomes an ambassador for the new women's American Basketball League

1997–Comes in second in the long jump at the U.S. Track and Field Championships in Indianapolis

Bibliography

Books

Anderson, Dave. *The Story of the Olympics.* New York: Beech Tree, 1996.

Benet, William Rose. *The Reader's Encyclopedia.* New York: Thomas Y. Crowell, 1965.

Cohen, Neil. *Jackie Joyner-Kersee: A Sports Illustrated Book for Kids.* New York: The Time Inc. Magazine Company, 1992.

Collins, Douglas. *Olympic Dreams, An Official Publication of the U.S. Olympics Committee.* New York: Universe, a division of Rizzoli International Publications, 1996.

Evslin, Bernard. *Heroes, Gods and Monsters of the Greek Myths.* New York: Bantam Books, 1975.

Goldstein, Margaret J., and Jennifer Larson. *Jackie Joyner-Kersee Superwoman.* Minneapolis: Lerner Publications Co., 1994.

Green, Carl R. *Jackie Joyner-Kersee.* New York: Crestwood House, Macmillan, 1994.

Green, Roger Lancelyn. *Tales of the Greek Heroes.* London: Penguin, 1988.

Harrington, Geri. *Jackie Joyner-Kersee, Champion Athlete.* New York: Chelsea House Publishers, 1995.

Jennings, Jay. *Teamwork: United in Victory.* Englewood Cliffs, New Jersey: Silver Burdett Press, 1990.

Laing, Jane, Sue Leonard, Christina Bankes, Mary Sutherland, Michael T. Wise, eds. *Chronicle of the Olympics.* London: Dorling Kindersley, 1996.

Leder, Jane. *Grace & Glory: A Century of Women in the Olympics.* Washington, D.C. and Chicago: Multi-Media Partners Ltd. and Triumph Books, 1996.

Plowden, Martha Ward. *Olympic Black Women.* Gretna, Louisiana: Pelican Publishing Company, 1996.

Rosenthal, Bert. *Track and Field: How To Play the All-Star Way.* Austin, Texas: Steck-Vaughn Company, 1994.

Sullivan, George. *Great Lives: Sports.* New York: Charles Scribner's Sons, 1988.

Magazine and Newspaper Articles

Adams, Kathleen, Charlotte Faltermayer, et al. "Olympics: The Agony of Victory." *Time* 11 Nov. 1996: 26.

Adler, Jerry. "The Dream Turns to Nightmare." *Newsweek* 5 Aug. 1996: 26.

"American Basketball League - Lady's Game." *Jet* 4 Nov. 1996: 47.

"America's Best Hopes." *U.S. News & World Report* 15 July 1996: 24.

Aubrey, Erin, and Eric Smith. "No More Singing the Blues." *Black Enterprise* Oct. 1996: 22.

"Betsy Makes a Famous Friend." *McCall's* March 1995: 157.

Chapell, Kevin. "The Awakening of the African Giant." *Ebony* Oct. 1996: 120.

Chetwynd, Josh. "Women Are Coming On Strong." *U.S. News & World Report* 24 March 1997: 10.

"Days of Wonder." *Newsweek* 5 Aug. 1996: 54.

Deford, Frank. "Jackie! Oh!" *Newsweek* 10 June 1996: 72.

———. "True Finishes." *Newsweek* 5 Aug. 1996: 50.

———. "Coming of Age in America." *Newsweek* 5 Aug. 1996: 38.

Dubin, Paula. "The First Lady of the Caribbean Cadences." *Americas* Jan./Feb. 1996: 36.

Edwards, Audrey. "The Age of Beauty." *Essence* Jan. 1995: 80.

"Fastest Dad." *Maclean's* 30 Sept. 1996: 29.

"50 Who Changed America." *Ebony* Nov. 1995: 108.

"First Lady of the Track." *TV Guide* 20 July 1996: 44.

"Great Olympic Moments." *Ebony* April 1992: 52.

"Hello, Dollies." *Life* Aug. 1994: 79.

"How Stars Overcame Obstacles." *Ebony* July 1995: 68.

"Jackie Passes Torch." *Jet* 17 June 1996: 48.

Kirkpatrick, Curry. "Monica's Dark Odyssey." *Newsweek* 4 Sept. 1995: 48.

Layden, Tim. "Thrills and Spills." *Sports Illustrated* 12 Aug. 1996: 34.

Leavy, Walter. "Blacks and the Biggest Olympics." *Ebony* Oct. 1996: 112.

"Lifetime McDonald's Treat." *Jet* 26 Aug. 1996: 59.

Longman, Jere. "Long-Jump Title Caps Jones's Double." *The New York Times* 16 June 1997: C10.

Malloy, Maria, and Erica Goode. "Izzy and the Party People." *U.S. News & World Report* 5 Aug. 1996: 156.

McCallum, Jack and Richard O'Brien. "No-shows Hurt the Show." *Sports Illustrated* 17 Feb. 1997: 20.

———— and Kostya Kennedy. "Bailey's Fine Whine." *Sports Illustrated* 13 Jan. 1997: 22.

McNally, Joe. "Naked Power, Amazing Grace." *Life* July 1996: 50.

"Meet the New Kick-butt Olympians." *Glamour* Aug. 1996: 95.

Mondi, Lawrence, and Kathleen Adams, et al. "Pentathlon: A Not-so-trivial Pursuit." *Time* 10 June 1996: 26.

Montville, Leigh. "Run for Your Life." *Sports Illustrated* 21 Oct. 1996: 72.

Moore, Kenny. "Coming on Strong." *Sports Illustrated* 5 Aug. 1996: 34.

——. "Head-to-head: Heike Drechsler vs. Jackie Joyner-Kersee." *Sports Illustrated* 22 July 1992: 66.

——. "Hot Stuff." *Sports Illustrated* 1 July 1996: 20.

Nemeth, Mary, James Deacon, et al. "Best in the World." *Maclean's* 12 Aug. 1996: 18.

"Olympic Gold Still Shining." *Good Housekeeping* Feb. 1992: 142.

"Prime Times." *Sports Illustrated* 24 June 1996: 34.

Rushin, Steve. "Playing with Heart." *Sports Illustrated* 29 July 1996: 54.

"Speed and Smiles." *Newsweek* 30 Dec. 1996: 63.

Starr, Mark. "Mr. Decathlon." *Newsweek* 1 July 1996: 66.

—— and Martha Bryant. "Gone with the Wind." *Newsweek* 12 Aug. 1996: 18.

"Track Star Jackie Joyner-Kersee Set to Play Professional Basketball." *Jet* 7 Oct. 1996: 48.

Werner, Laurie. "The Moment I Knew I Was a Mom." *Parents* May 1995: 83.

Wilson-Smith, Anthony. "Triumph and Tragedy." *Maclean's* 5 Aug. 1996: 10.

"Women of Distinction." *Ebony Man* Nov. 1993: 50.

"Women's Track & Field." *U.S. News & World Report* 15 July 1996: 55.

Wulf, Steve. "Double Fast." *Time* 12 Aug. 1996: 44.

Zoglin, Richard. "The Girls of Summer." *Time* 12 Aug. 1996: 49.

Photo Credits